Ratha and Thistle-chaser

ALSO BY CLARE BELL

RATHA'S CREATURE
CLAN GROUND
TOMORROW'S SPHINX

Ratha and Thistle-chaser

CLARE BELL

Margaret K. McElderry Books

NEW YORK

Margaret K. McElderry Books
Macmillan Publishing Company
866 Third Avenue
New York, New York 10022
Collier Macmillan Canada, Inc.

First Edition
Printed in the United States of America
10 9 8 7 6 5 4 3 2 1

Library of Congress Cataloging-in-Publication Data
Bell, Clare.
Ratha and Thistle-chaser / Clare Bell. — 1st ed.
p. cm.
Summary: Crippled and tortured by paralyzing nightmares, Newt, a
solitary cat, finds a new life for herself with the strange tusked
creatures of the seashore until her peaceful existence is disrupted
by Ratha's scout Thakur, who brings welcome companionship but also
forces Newt to face her terrifying past.
[1. Fantasy. 2. Cats—Fiction.] I. Title.
PZ7.B3889153Ras 1990   [Fic]—dc20   89–36807   CIP   AC
ISBN 0-689-50462-4

Ratha and
Thistle-chaser

CHAPTER 1

ON MATTED, shadow-laced grass in a forest clearing, two wild cats quarreled over prey. They made threat-growls as each circled the other. One was the size and weight of a panther, with a faded dun coat and a ribby, rickety look that spoke his age. The other, a female, was a strange mix of rust brown mottled with orange. A black mask across her face gave emphasis to her chalk-green eyes. Her youth might have given her the advantage despite her smallness, but her left foreleg was withered and drawn up against her chest.

With her pelt of rusty black and orange and her slow uncertain manner, she resembled a newt, an eellike creature with legs. Once those of her own kind had cruelly kicked a dead one at her, as if to show her what she was. Perhaps they were right. Often she felt as dazed and bewildered as a newt that had crawled from its clammy hole into bright sun.

She remembered the dead thing—cold, limp, and coated with slime that made it too noxious for even her to eat. It was then that the image wormed itself into her mind. From that time, she thought of herself as Newt.

Her gaze fastened on the dusty feathered bundle pinned

beneath the old dun-coat's claws. It wasn't a fresh catch; her nose told her that the bird had been dead for days. The paw claiming it trembled with age and weakness. The grizzled head bent to strip away feathers.

She gathered her three good legs beneath her, preparing for a rush that would bowl the ancient male over. Carrion rank as this had repulsed her in better days. Now her belly was shrunken, and the odor of any kind of food made her drool.

The dun-coat lifted his head, fixing watery yellow eyes on her. He made sounds that were more than just growls or whines. The sounds and the way he lashed his tail created feelings inside Newt that she didn't want. She knew the old male despised her.

His noises made her feel just what she was: Ugly. Dull.

The old dun-coat tore at the rotten bird. Newt's other feelings gave way to her fierce hunger. She lunged, driving into him and knocking him to the ground. He collapsed like the bundle of sticks he resembled. She sank her teeth into the prize and lifted it. He was struggling to his feet again, making mewling sounds.

He faced her so that she looked him full in the eyes. She met there the things she had seen in the gaze of others, but somehow his outraged stare was stronger. It asked questions—questions she could not answer.

What are you that you would take the last scrap of meat from a dying old one? Have you no respect for the ending of life . . . ?

The message came not in sounds but in the fierce look from those watery yellow-green eyes. She wanted to flee with the ragged carcass, but the elder's stare held her. And, as she was imprisoned by his gaze and her growing shame and confusion, his eyes seemed to change before her, becoming those of one she knew well and hated. From somewhere behind her own eyes, inside her own skull, a familiar nightmare swept down on her. She heard rushing, pounding, and an echoing growl that rose to a shriek. In her fevered vision, a cat-shaped apparition rose up before her with gleaming fangs. The flame-colored demon stabbed its teeth into her crippled shoulder and foreleg, waking the old pain. She struggled, but in the vision she was always smaller, weaker, unable to defend herself. The dream-creature seized her, tore her, and then threw her aside into an abyss, where she lay until the blackness lightened.

Newt woke on her side, bleakly aware that she had fallen once again into the grip of her strange sickness. Now the Dreambiter was gone. Episodes like this were half seizure, half nightmare, and totally bewildering. She found herself still moving her legs weakly. Taking deep breaths, she quieted her movements.

As her heartbeat slowed, she pulled her feet beneath her and rolled onto her chest. She waited, dreading the light-headedness that might herald another attack. Often the dream and the illness would return, savaging her a second or third time before releasing her.

This time there was no sudden relapse. She stumbled to her feet, the contracted muscles in her crippled limb pulling as she mistakenly tried to use the leg. Her nightmare was gone. So was the old male and his feathered carrion. Newt sighed, knowing he had been able to stagger a safe distance away while she thrashed helplessly. Yet the memory of him shamed her a little less, perhaps because she knew he would have at least one more meal.

But why care about the old dun-coat? Usually she wouldn't. It was too hard to think about anything except scratching up something to eat when she could no longer bear the pain of hunger. But sometimes other thoughts and feelings thrust themselves into her narrow world, like those the old one had roused in her, making her care or shaming her because she didn't.

Newt hung her head, not wanting this hateful clarity of mind that came to her briefly on these occasions and added to her wretchedness. Yet, perhaps she was capable of thoughts beyond the bare needs of survival. She already knew the difference between kindness and cruelty, for she had felt both at some time in her dim past.

She shook her head to drive out some of the lingering dizziness. Sometimes it seemed as though the mist that always fogged her mind might lift, letting her think clearly. There had been a time . . . once . . . before the Dreambiter . . .

No. She wasn't going to think about her nightmare. It might rise again, battering her from within.

Slowly, awkwardly, Newt turned. With her useless foreleg tucked up beneath her chest, she limped downhill.

A fresh wind blew from beyond the trees, bringing a sea smell to Newt's nose and a fresh pang of hunger to her belly. She rarely went that way, for she was reluctant to leave the shelter of the forest. But now, frustration and self-pity made her reckless.

The smell teased her, hinting that she might find something washed ashore that she could gnaw on. It sparked a memory, flickering, but strong enough to draw her. A memory of feathers scattered on sand, bleached to brittleness by the salt wind. Of fragile bones splintering between her teeth, releasing crumbled marrow. Shards of flesh, salt encrusted and hard as the bones that softened in her mouth and released an echo of flavor before they slipped down her throat and were gone.

The trees thinned to scrub, and the soil became stony beneath her feet as Newt left the forest for the coast. She hesitated, leaning forward on her good forepaw and switching her tail. Cries and wingbeats overhead made her shoulders hunch. Birds with tapered wings, gray backs, and plump white bellies soared above her. She slunk through sedge grass to low, broken cliffs that over-looked the beach.

There she crouched, feeling the wind lift the fur on the back of her neck and tease the tips of her ears. Lifting her muzzle, she tested the wind. There were queer smells of animals and other things, but no scents of her own kind. She was alone on the clifftop.

She listened to the crash and roll of the surf below. Then she threaded her way down across crumbling bluffs until her paws broke the sand-crust at the top of the beach. For a moment, she retreated, puzzled by the way the sand gave beneath her when she tried to walk on it.

She ventured out once again, feeling the loose sand grind between her pads and drag at her legs, making her limping pace more awkward than ever. For a moment, she looked back up the tumbled slope, wondering if she should turn around. Retreating was the easy thing to do. She had done it most of her life.

Perhaps something in the brisk wind challenged Newt this time. Drawing her whiskers back, she lowered her head and slogged through the crusted sand. She passed a line of sea wrack and nosed among the drying kelp and gull feathers for carrion but found nothing. Hordes of sand fleas scattered in front of her as she made her way down onto the hard-packed sand near the surf line.

The endless march of waves breaking on shore drew and held her gaze. The roar and boom of the surf and the salt spray blowing into her face seemed to dash away some of the confusion that lay like a gray mist over her mind. Frothy water slithered up the beach and spilled onto her toes, drawing the sand from under her pads as it retreated.

She wasn't sure if the wind blowing in her face or the water stroking her toes bothered her or not. At least this place of water and sand did not demand anything of her.

Swinging her tail, Newt hobbled along the damp sand just beyond the surf line. She squinted against sunglare and the spray that stiffened the fur on her face. Looking back, she saw the wandering trail of her footprints. In the forest she would have scuffed them out, but here it didn't seem to matter. The slow crash and hiss of the sea lulled her, and she walked as if in a trance, feeling the sun on her back and the wind in her ears.

Newt's good forepaw struck a rock and she stumbled, falling onto her chest. Irritated and impatient with her clumsiness, she scrambled up and looked around. She had to turn her head to take in her surroundings, for her vision had tunneled, as it often did when she became frightened or angry. She hated that, for it felt as if the world had shrunk to only the small space in front of her, leaving the rest to be engulfed by blackness. And sometimes that small space would retreat far away, and then the Dreambiter would come.

She shook herself fiercely, as if she could free herself of the hateful vision the way she did the sand in her coat. The cool freshness of the wind in her face helped. Gradually her vision opened once again, and the warning throb in the back of her head faded. Now she could see that she had come to a low shelf of gray mudstone, dotted with embedded shells and filled with shallow potholes. She hopped up and sniffed at a shallow tidepool. Several flowerlike objects beneath the surface startled her by withdrawing their narrow petals and huddling into gray-green lumps.

Intrigued, she poked at them with her good forepaw while she lay on her side, trying to get them to emerge and wave about again, but they remained sullenly closed. She got up and went on.

Newt had come to a terraced area beneath a low cliff where slabs of mudstone formed a series of shelves stepping down to the sea. The tidepools on the higher shelves held only more reclusive water flowers and a few empty shells. The lower pools lay near enough to the waves to fill as the surf rushed in and drain when the water retreated.

The brine swirled high around her legs and splashed her belly as she investigated these pools, and she found them filled with swimming, scuttling, and crawling creatures. Spiny sculpins eyed her from niches between rocks. Little crabs danced away sideways when her shadow fell on them. Pearl-shelled snails, waving their horns, glided over mats of purple algae.

She waded from one tidepool to another, her sudden fascination with the inhabitants not just the result of curiosity. The rockfish looked as if they could provide a few bites of food. The seasnails were much easier to catch, but their shells were tough and weren't as easily cracked as the more fragile shells of land snails. She nearly broke a back tooth trying to crack one and at last spat it out in disgust.

Newt noticed that each wave seemed to roll in farther than before, slowly submerging the lower tidepools. She wasn't ready to leave yet; she had spied a big sculpin lurking at the bottom of a brine-filled crevice. Settling herself on her side, she plunged her good forepaw into the water after the fish. It scooted away much faster than its large head and clumsy fins had suggested it could. She made another swipe. The fish evaded her, slipping tail first into the deepest part of the crevice and making pop eyes at her. An attempt to claw the sculpin out ended when its spines pierced her pawpad.

With a dismayed yowl, Newt pulled her paw out and floundered away, leaving the tidepools to the rising water. She scrambled over the mudstone terraces back to the beach, her stomach still grumbling and her pricked forepaw stinging.

Feeling vulnerable, she sought shelter in a cave beneath an outcrop of sandstone. She collapsed on her side, brought her bleeding pad to her face, and licked it. A vague sense of dread came over her. With one foreleg crippled, even a minor injury to the other could keep her immobilized, unable to hunt for food or fresh water.

A dull sense of outrage made her bare her teeth and flatten her ears. She whimpered—and trembled at the sound of despair in her own voice. Laying her cheek down on her throbbing forepaw, she sought sleep but found only a fitful doze.

The Dreambiter came, not in a rush and hiss as it had before, but quietly, stealing up behind misted half-dreams. It was huge, and Newt was tiny. Sometimes the Dreambiter wore a pelt of flames, but this time it was a shadow, lit from behind by the colors of sunset. Only the eyes shimmered green, and the look in them was not hatred but anguish.

Newt knew a moment of pity for the Dreambiter, but that instant fled as blood-red light caught and stained the apparition's fangs. The teeth plunged into her flesh and kept going, striking deep into the center of her soul, ripping a shriek from her throat. Pain bloomed like an ugly flower, grew and grew until she thought even in her dream that this was the end and that the Dreambiter would take her.

But it was a dream, and although the vision could give pain, it could not give death. The final injustice was that she did wake, only to find the bleak landscape of her life before her once again. Ghost-pain danced through her neck and shoulder, through the scars of the old bite, and out into her contracted foreleg, making the stiff muscles spasm. She rolled on the leg to ease the cramping.

Lying on the sand in her shallow little cave beneath the overhang, she tried not to think of anything at all. Often her mind would oblige her by going completely blank, but this time it dwelled on her nightmare. There was something about her memory of the moment before the Dreambiter's attack that tormented her. In the vision she turned into someone smaller, weaker, yet more agile and not burdened by a lamed foreleg. And there was a difference in her mind too, for she sensed, though only fleetingly, that her thoughts at that time were not as blurred or misted by confusion as they were now. She had been whole; now she was broken. The Dreambiter had destroyed more than just her front leg.

Newt woke from a sleep she had no memory of entering. The pain in her leg had faded, to be replaced by restlessness. She tried out her spine-pricked paw and found that the fire had gone down to a dull ache. Slowly she limped northward up the beach.

High tide covered mudflats and shell beds in the cliff shadow near a river mouth. As she wandered, skirting waves that broke high on the flats, she heard a grinding sound followed by snuffles and snorts. She halted, swiveling her ears. A fishy sea-animal odor teased her nose. Then another scent came, mixed in with the wind. Newt couldn't identify it, but there was a meaty odor that hinted at food.

Her reflexive swallow started her stomach churning and cramping. She had been about to withdraw, but now, driven by hunger, she had to go on. She limped toward the noise.

In the frothing shallow water covering the flats, Newt caught sight of an animal that was totally strange to her. It looked immense, whiskered and blubbery. Creases formed in the rolls of fat around its neck as it swung its head from side to side. Its muzzle was wide and pushed in. Short but massive tusks protruded from beneath a loose, slobbery upper lip.

As she watched, taking in the details of the animal's appearance, she wished she could capture the impression in a way that would keep the images in her mind from fading. She sensed that such a way existed, though she didn't know what it was. Another of her kind had once tried to teach her.

A memory came to her, a picture of a copper-furred face with amber eyes. She remembered a warm tongue that washed her, a male scent, and a deep purring voice. And then the face in her mind started to move, the mouth opening and making sounds. The same sounds came repeatedly until the thought had risen in her mind that the sounds were supposed to mean something. And she had been on the verge of understanding them just as the Dreambiter had attacked, driving the kind one away and burying her dawning awareness under an avalanche of pain.

Yet that memory remained of a gentle voice trying to encourage, to teach. She opened her own mouth, startling herself by making a noise between a growl and a whimper.

The strangeness in her voice frightened her. The edges of her vision started to close in. The Dreambiter stirred but did not rise. Newt's fear gradually faded.

She became aware of the sea-creature staring at her. It humped itself farther inshore and began raking a submerged shell bed with its tusks. Each time the water receded, exposing shellfish, more of the fleshy food-smell drifted downwind, drawing Newt closer. At first the blubbery, tusked beast seemed to have no legs at all, but then she caught sight of a stumpy, flippered forelimb. The creature itself had an oily stink that caught in Newt's throat and made her grimace, but the aroma coming from the crushed shellfish enticed her.

With a startled grunt, the blubber-tusker heaved itself upright and stared at her with eyes spaced so far apart they seemed about to fall off the sides of its pug-nosed face. She could see its nostrils twitch as it caught her scent. The hair rose on her nape.

The blubber-tusker lowered its head, lumbering a few paces back. Emboldened by the animal's retreat, Newt started forward. One step at a time, she limped down the sloping flats, trembling with hunger. She had almost reached the shell bed when the creature bellowed and wriggled toward her, its heaving motion sending ripples through its blubber.

On three legs, Newt scampered shoreward, terrified that her pursuer was about to catch her. Instead the beast had come to a stop, puffing and blowing. It slapped the water with a stumpy hind flipper, roaring at her. Newt's first reaction was surprise. Here was a creature that she could actually outrun, even at her limping pace.

The realization gave her courage, and instead of hobbling away, she stayed, watching the blubber-tusker shake its fat neck at her. Again she ventured nearer, ignoring the animal's deafening roars. She nosed the edge of a broken clamshell, tasting what was inside. A shock of delight went through her when the meaty flavor spread over her tongue. In a sudden frenzy, she attacked the shell bed, clawing open damaged shells and swallowing the rubbery meat inside, nearly breaking her fangs in the rush.

A splashing, roaring commotion sent her scooting away, a clamshell still wedged in her jaws. In her urge to eat as much as she could, she had forgotten the blubber-tusker. Again she kept well away from the creature's lumbering charge, and it halted, quivering, blowing out through its whiskers in frustration.

Newt waited until it had gone back to raking the shell

bed before she mounted her next raid. The fact that the huge beast was slower than she was gave her a mischievous joy. She spent the afternoon scavenging from the plundered shell beds and dodging the walrus. At last it lumbered seaward, dived into a wave, and was gone.

As sunset streaked the beach in silver and gold, Newt padded back to the cave where she had napped. Her belly was full enough to ease hunger cramps, though this food was different from anything she had eaten before, and her stomach gurgled.

When she reached her cave, it looked much friendlier. With food in her belly and less pain in her foot, her mind felt clearer. She decided that she disliked the beach less than other places. For the present, this part of it was hers. She limped backward until her tail lay against a block of sandstone and sprayed the rock with her scent.

Newt flattened her ears and snaked her head back and forth, suddenly fearing that someone would come and take this place from her. She waited, stiff and tense. Nothing happened. Waves rolled in and washed out. Birds drifted down the sky with distant calls.

She crawled into the cave, making a nest for herself in the warm sand. She wondered if the tusked sea-animal would return to the shell beds, and while she was wondering, drowsiness crept over her, drew her head down on her paw, and coaxed her into sleep.

CHAPTER 2

RATHA, THE LEADER of the Named, squinted through the trees to a sun paled by blowing dust. She had grit in her fawn-colored pelt, in the fur of her tail, and between the toes of all four paws. Her tongue felt dry and sticky against her fangs. On the riverbank where she stood, three-horn deer and small dapplebacked horses milled in groups, guarded by her people. The Named had long ago given up the risky life of hunters for the more stable existence of herders, living on the meat of the beasts they kept.

Many of the Named carried a small companion called a treeling on their backs: a lemurlike creature with large eyes, a pointed muzzle, a ringed tail, and hands instead of paws. The treelings were the descendants of a single female who had been adopted by one of the Named as a pet. Her hands had proved useful for tasks too difficult for claws or teeth.

Ratha had her own treeling, a female called Ratharee, who sat on her back and groomed her. She felt deft treeling fingers comb the fur along her spine. Ratharee seemed to know exactly where the fleas tickled and would groom there before Ratha twitched or scratched. Sometimes Ratha felt needle-sharp teeth as the treeling nibbled to dislodge a stubborn tick, but Ratharee never nipped her.

Ratha turned her attention to the animals. The dapplebacks stood with their three-toed forefeet in the sluggish flow, nuzzling the water and sucking it up with thirsty gulps. Ratha badly wanted a bath, but she knew she'd have to settle for licking herself with her tongue. The river was too shallow to do more than wet her belly.

At least it had some water. The brook that ran from the river through the home pastures had become a dry channel, forcing the Named to move their drinking site.

Every day the water supply dwindled as the river fell. It was so low now that the three-horns and dapplebacks could not be watered together, or their hooves would churn mud into the water, making it undrinkable. Ratha watched as Named herders held the animals together by circling them, snarling and showing teeth. Firekeepers took up outlying positions, some carrying torches bearing the fire-creature called the Red Tongue. In good times, when the meadow brook ran full and clear and the pasturage was lush, herders rarely displayed more than an irritated grimace to control the animals, and the Red Tongue was needed only to defend themselves against outside raids. Now thirst made the herdbeasts restive, irritable, likely to rebel or stampede. The herders needed the Firekeepers close by, backing up the threat of claws and teeth with the threat of fire.

The dapplebacks grunted and squealed, laying back their ears, shaking their stiff, short manes, and lashing out with hoofed toes at any herder not quick enough to evade their ill temper. Ratha's flank still stung from an unexpected kick.

She gave a soft *prrrup* that brought Ratharee from her back onto the nape of her neck. The treeling chirred and draped herself so that her forelegs and muzzle lay along the slant of one feline shoulder, while rear legs and tail extended along the other. The treeling angled her nose out, watching the commotion. Perhaps, Ratha thought, Ratharee was looking at her own treeling offspring, who now rode the backs of young herders.

Ratha paced the bank as the clan rounded up the dapplebacks that had already drunk, clearing the way for a group of three-horn does and fawns. She saw Thakur, the herding teacher, dodge a charge from a thirsty doe who threatened him with its forked nose-horn. His treeling, Aree, leaped from his scruff into the air in front of the deer, screeching and flailing her ringed tail. The startled herdbeast jumped sideways, its charge broken. Thakur and the others moved the does in to drink.

A grunting bellow rose above the tumult of lowing and bawling herdbeasts. Ratharee, startled, clung tightly to Ratha's neck as the largest three-horn stag broke loose from the herd and headed for the river.

Snarling, Ratha leaped to join other herders dashing to cut the beast off. She found Thakur galloping alongside her through the scattered trees that edged the river. His copper coat flashed as he ran through patches of sun and shade with Aree riding on his nape.

"Turn the stag!" the herding teacher yowled. "Don't try to block him!" Ratha saw Fessran, the Firekeeper leader, join the fray. A torch flame roared at the end of the branch in Fessran's jaws. Close behind ran Bira, a red-gold shadow to Fessran's sand-colored pelt.

Ratha skidded to a stop to let Ratharee scramble off.

The treeling bounced on her hind legs over to Bira and jumped on alongside Bira's own companion.

"Stay behind, Firekeepers," Ratha called as she raced between saplings. The fire-creature she called the Red Tongue could cow aggressive animals, but the Named used it only if they had no other way.

She and Thakur turned the three-horn stag in tighter circles until it danced and bucked, pivoting on its hind feet to meet the herders with head horns and jabbing at them with both prongs of the forked nose-horn. The stag paused in its flurry, snorting and panting. Ratha saw her chance.

She lunged toward the three-horn stag, stamping with both forepaws together. She caught its gaze, locked her own with the animal's. The three-horn bellowed, shook its heavy neck, but could not look away. Ratha took another step toward the beast, intensifying her stare. She put all her will into it, menacing and hypnotizing the beast.

She took another slow step, holding her body low, bowing her back, hunching her shoulders. Memories of a similar incident edged into her mind, threatening to distract her. Once, when she had been Thakur's student, she had confronted a defiant three-horn. That time she allowed her gaze to break, and the animal nearly trampled her.

From behind her came the soft hiss of the Red Tongue as it fluttered on Fessran's torch. The power was there, if she wanted or needed it. But the Red Tongue was too savage a thing to be used lightly when dealing with herdbeasts. Brought too close, it could madden them, and the only choice then was a quick, killing bite. She didn't want to sacrifice the stag now, even though the Named needed the meat. It was a bad time and place; the other animals were too restive.

Even so, the instinct to attack rose up in her, almost overwhelming her need to approach slowly, eyes fixed on the quarry. She fought down an urge to spring that tightened her muscles like a cramp. She knew that to return the stag safely to the herd, she must master it by the strength of her gaze. Her stare never faltered or wavered, holding the beast until its proud head dropped in defeat.

Ratha let out her breath as Ratharee came scampering back to her and clambered on. Other herders led the stag back to the herd. She shook herself, sneezed dust from her nose.

Thakur trotted up, his green eyes glowing in his copper-furred face. His treeling, Aree, was Ratharee's mother. He had originally brought Aree to the clan as a pet.

"Well, yearling," Thakur said, using his old teasing name for Ratha, "that was one of the best stare-downs I've seen."

"We need every skilled herder we have," Ratha answered, warmed by his praise. "Even me." Her tail twitched. "And Shongshar's rise taught me what can happen if I forget that I am also one of the clan and must work among our people to understand our needs."

She paced back between the trees with Ratharee on her shoulder, thinking about Shongshar, the orange-eyed stranger she had admitted into the clan. His mating with Bira had produced cubs lacking the intelligence and self-awareness that the Named valued, and Ratha had been forced to exile those youngsters so that they would not grow up in the clan. Embittered by the loss, Shongshar had turned against her, using the Red Tongue to create a worshipful following among the Firekeepers that was strong enough to cast her down from leadership and out of the clan.

It had been two summers since Ratha had fought to gain back her position, but the Named had been long in recovering. Some, like the Firekeeper leader, Fessran, still bore scars on their pelts from Shongshar's long fangs. Fessran had sided with the Firekeepers and Shongshar in the struggle two summers ago. But when Shongshar held Ratha down for the killing bite, Fessran flung herself between the two, taking the wound. Ratha had escaped his saber-teeth, but her memory of him would never fade from her mind and only gradually from those of her people. And now, too soon after that wrenching time, the drought had come.

The Named watered their herdbeasts with no more major incidents and drove them to a nearby clearing that still had scattered grass and a few thickets with green leaves. Ratha lay down in the shade, missing the sunning rock that stood in the middle of clan ground. She liked to lie on the sunning rock, looking out over the beasts and herders. But now, though spring had not yet yielded to summer, the brook running through the old pasture had dried up, and the green faded into gold and brown.

And how long would the river itself last? Each day it shrank, and the net of cracks in the muddy banks grew and deepened. Ratha remembered tales told by elders of seasons when the Named had left clan ground in a search for pasturage and water. But it had been so long ago that no one could recall where they went or how they managed.

As the animals straggled past, she watched dappleback foals capering about their mothers. Fewer had been born this dry spring. Among the three-horns, several fawns butted and nuzzled at the dams' flanks. Three-horns often had twins, but this season none of the does had dropped more than one fawn, as if their bodies sensed that they would have food and milk to rear only a single youngster.

Ratha tipped her head back to eye the sun's white-gold fire against a bleached sky. If rain came again, even a little, the forage might recover enough to last through the summer. But nothing could be done to recover from the disappointment of spring breeding. The herds would decrease instead of expanding this year. Still, if the Named limited the number of their own new cubs, perhaps they could live on what they had.

Ratha gave a soft snort at her own presumption. If there was anything she couldn't control, it was the fertility of Named females. Though the clan's mating season had been delayed by the hardships of a dry winter and spring, it would still come. And, if things went as they had the last breeding time, she herself wouldn't be adding to the number of new cubs.

In a way she felt relieved. Watching mothers cope with their litters of squalling, scrambling youngsters made her feel tired, and the occasional times she did nursery duty, her patience was gone long before someone rescued her. It was clear she was not fit for motherly duties. Still . . .

Stop dreaming, she told herself crossly. *You had your chance, and look what happened.* She sighed. Every once in a while thoughts of her lost litter by the Un-Named male, whom she called Bonechewer, still entered her mind. The Un-Named were those of Ratha's kind who lived outside the clan. Though they resembled her people so closely that they could mate with the Named, they lacked the spark of self-awareness that made thought and language possible. Or so Ratha had believed until her banishment for daring to challenge clan leadership with the Red Tongue, the fire-creature she had found. Her exile forced her to live among the Un-Named, and there she met Bonechewer, an intelligent male with the ability to speak. He and Ratha had mated.

By now she should have forgotten, but images of the cubs, especially of her daughter, Thistle-chaser, still haunted her. She remembered Thistle-chaser's beautiful empty eyes, which spoke of a mind too stunted to know the world in the way the Named did.

I wonder where she is now. I remember Bonechewer said she lived to run with the Un-Named. Ratha sighed, blowing the breath out between her front fangs and startling Ratharee. Long ago she had dismissed any thought of trying to find the cubs. What good would it do her, or them either? She would look at their eyes and the old rage would rekindle, the fury of knowing that her flesh and blood were nothing more than animals like the herdbeasts on which she fed or the marauders she fought, or the treeling she carried on her back. Even Ratharee's eyes held more flickerings of the mind's light than her sons' and daughter's ever would.

She tore herself away from the bleak landscape of her memory and gazed out at the herders, their beasts, and their treelings. They were her sons and daughters now —all those who made up the clan, all those who knew names and their worth. She sighted along her nose to a distant point where a fire burned with a Firekeeper standing watch nearby. This too was her progeny, this flame-creature called the Red Tongue, with its power to twist and sear those who bore it. If she had known of this when she first found the Red Tongue, would she have brought it back as a gift to her people? She shivered again with the memory of Shongshar and the struggle between herders and Firekeepers that nearly destroyed the Named.

Now she was wiser. One like Shongshar would never again rise within the clan, not while she had wit and strength to prevent it.

Ratharee rubbed her small head against Ratha's cheek, as if reminding her of the unexpected gift those events had brought: the coming of Ratharee and her kind. If Thakur hadn't found that injured treeling cub, or if he had found it and decided to eat it . . .

She glanced to one side, catching a flicker of motion in the corner of one eye. Thakur, the clan herding teacher, was trotting toward her with Aree bouncing on his shoulder.

"Are the beasts settled?" she called to him.

"Yes, now that they've drunk. I'm glad you decided to stay near the river." He lay down beside her and licked dust from his copper fur.

"I'm worried, herding teacher," Ratha said. "You know how few young herdbeasts were born this season. We will have to limit the number we use for meat."

"There won't be enough," Thakur said, looking at her steadily.

"I know. We can't depend on the herdbeasts entirely for food. Later there may be other food, such as those soggy fruit-things the treelings eat. I know you like fruits, but my stomach won't stand them." She paused. "The Named used to hunt all kinds of animals. Perhaps some of those that we used to hunt we can learn to herd. It wasn't that long ago that old Baire brought three-horns to us."

"I remember when a certain three-horn stag chased a young herding student up a tree." Thakur's eyes glowed with amusement at this memory of Ratha. "But you are right, clan leader. We have overlooked other animals. We should keep creatures that can do well in dry seasons, as well as those that flourish in good times."

"This is what I will do," said Ratha finally. "I will call all the strong, young herders and Firekeepers to the sunning rock. Those I need to guard the animals and the Red Tongue on our lands I will send back to their posts. Those who remain will stand in pairs in a circle with their backs to me and their noses pointed outward. Each pair will travel in the direction they face, seeking a place with water and forage for our herds, as well as new beasts we can learn to keep."

"You know that the mating season will soon come, even if it is short," said Thakur. "I heard Fessran yowling last night. I don't think she was just singing."

"With fewer of the Named on clan land during the mating season, fewer cubs will be born, I hope."

"Perhaps that is sad, clan leader, but it is wise," answered Thakur. "And I will also take my place among those you send."

Ratha was unsure how to respond to Thakur's offer. She found herself starting to lick a paw and scrub her face to avoid answering him.

"Yearling," he said, using his old teasing name for her again, "I leave the clan every mating season. You know why, and I thought my going no longer bothered you."

She licked her pad and gave her cheek a harder swipe than she meant to. "You won't sire empty-eyed cubs on me, if that's what you fear. I have not birthed cubs by anyone since Bonechewer. The matings don't take."

Thakur looked at the ground. "It is not just you I worry about, Ratha. The others too—Bira, Fessran. They don't think about such things when the mating fever takes them. If I stay, the risk of siring witless cubs remains."

Ratha knew what he said was true, and a part of her cried out in sorrow for him. He would never take a mate from among the Named and risk fathering young on a clan female.

Thakur, along with Bonechewer, who was his brother and had lived with the Un-Named, had been born from a mating between a clan female called Reshara and an Un-Named male. Both brothers possessed gifts, showing that such pairings could produce cubs with the light of intelligence in their eyes. But the results were too erratic to trust and too tragic to risk.

Though Thakur knew only that Ratha had birthed Bonechewer's cubs and lost them, he did not know why. But he had witnessed the results of another mating between one of the Named and an Un-Named outsider.

Shongshar's cubs by Bira had lacked the ability to speak and think that the Named so valued. Thakur knew that well, for he had helped Ratha carry both litterlings from clan ground.

Thakur nosed Ratha gently, mistaking the reason for

her mood. "Don't mourn because you have no young, clan leader. We, the Named, are your cubs. And I also have sons and daughters in the young ones who learn the ways of herding from me."

The treeling on his shoulder chirred, as if to remind him that she too was part of his adopted kin. Ratha's small companion, Ratharee, trilled back at her mother.

"When those who are to journey take their places, let me choose where I will stand," Thakur asked. "And let me go by myself, as I always do."

"Do you know where you want to go?"

"Yes. I will stand and lift my head to place the setting sun at my whisker-tips. It will lead me to a place I have seen only once, from a distance, to a body of water greater than any lake."

"Then I will have the gathering at sunset, and you will choose your place," Ratha answered, her head full of the pictures Thakur's words conjured. She felt a prick of envy, wishing she could travel with him, leaving behind the burden of leadership. But he would return and perhaps take her with him to see what he had found, though not for a while. She watched him pad away with Aree on his back, his tail swinging. She wished he didn't remind her so much of Bonechewer, the father of her own lost cubs.

In the midafternoon heat Ratha ambled instead of trotted as she made her rounds among the scattered beasts, herders, and Firekeepers. At the nearest guard-fire, she saw Fessran. A tickle of worry about her friend crept along her back. The Firekeeper leader had seemed subdued lately.

Ratha touched noses and rubbed the full length of her body against her friend, crooking her tail over Fessran's back. She could tell by the warm tone in Fessran's scent that the Firekeeper welcomed such open affection. But underneath, Fessran's smell told Ratha her friend was troubled.

"Thakur says he heard you singing last night," Ratha said, trying to tease. "It is known among the Named that when Fessran is in full voice, the mating season is not far behind."

Fessran's reply was flat. "Thakur must have his ears stuffed with herdbeast hair. That was Bira, not me."

Ratha's ears swiveled forward, and she tried to look into Fessran's eyes as the Firekeeper asked, "No one's been complaining about me, have they? I mean, I haven't shirked my duties even while I've been looking for my treeling."

"No," Ratha answered. She felt her own companion on her shoulder. Fessran looked a bit scruffy. Ever since her Fessree had disappeared, she had to depend on her own tongue for grooming.

"Do you want to borrow Ratharee?" Ratha asked.

"No. I appreciate the offer, but grooming isn't the same if another treeling does it." Fessran let her forepaws slide out until her creamy belly fur flattened the grass. "Funny. I never thought I'd really get attached to the little flea-picker. You and Thakur are as soft as dung when it comes to treelings, but I thought I was being more practical about it. It's not Fessree's little hands I miss. It's her sitting on my shoulder and making noises in my ear. I got used to it."

Ratha saw her shift some of the weight off her left foreleg, rolling half onto her side.

"How is your leg?"

"Thanks to Shongshar, it'll never be the same again, even though it's had this long to heal. I should be grateful that it works at all. Shoulder's just a bit stiff. Bites heal better when you're younger." She licked the two puckered scars on her upper foreleg. There was another set of scars on her ribs where Shongshar's saber-teeth had emerged through the leg and into her chest. It was a near-fatal wound, and Ratha was amazed and grateful Fessran had healed this well. Although Bira was coming along as Fessran's backup for Firekeeper leader, Ratha needed Fessran in that role.

"You know, I wouldn't feel so bad about Fessree," Ratha said in an attempt to sound comforting. "Treelings sometimes wander off, but they come back. Aree did that to Thakur."

"Well, I thought it might be because of the mating season. Everybody's smell changing and all that. I notice it makes treelings nervous." Fessran fell silent for a minute, but her scent told Ratha that she wasn't in heat and probably wouldn't be this season. After her wound and the long recovery that followed, she wasn't yet in condition to bear a litter.

"You know why I'm so caught up with that miserable flea-picker?" Fessran asked suddenly, after a long silence. "It's because of Nyang."

Nyang. For a moment Ratha switched her tail, lost. Nyang was dead. He had been Fessran's eldest cub from her last litter, one of those who went over to Shongshar when the clan split into two factions. He had been drowned when Ratha and Thakur managed to flood out the cave where Shongshar had hidden his worship-fire. In helping Ratha to dig the trench that diverted the stream from its banks, Fessran had helped in her son's death.

"I don't know why it's bothering me. I still have Khushi and Chita, though they both are grown. I never felt I knew Nyang as well as I did the others. And then he was gone, and I lost my chance. Well, it's foolish to mourn now."

"No, it isn't foolish at all," said Ratha, thinking of her own daughter, Thistle-chaser.

Fessran stared at her paws. "After his death I kept thinking of Nyang until it hurt too much. And then Fessree started grooming me very gently and saying tree-ling nonsense in my ear, and it helped."

"I know."

Fessran lifted her muzzle abruptly, startling Ratha. "Do you really know, Ratha? Or would you like me to believe you know? Even though you are clan leader, you still seem so young to me. Have you ever felt the pain of losing a cub you birthed?"

Ratha closed her eyes, trying to keep Thistle-chaser's story from rushing onto her tongue. No one knew about her lost litter except Thakur, and it was something best kept to herself. Besides, what good would it do to tell except to raise her own old pain again? Fessran didn't need that. What she wanted was strength from her clan leader, not weakness.

Instead Ratha said, "If it will help, Thakur and I will search for Fessree."

Fessran hauled herself to her feet, trying not to favor her shoulder. "I've been everywhere. It's easier to see into the treetops now that the leaves are shriveling in the drought. No. You're both busy. I'll just leave Fessree to herself, the ungrateful bug-eater."

She got up and walked off, swinging her tail. Ratha sat at the foot of the sunning rock, looking after her and wondering what else she could have said. Fessran's change in mood had caught her by surprise, thrown her off balance. The accusation against her of immaturity and lack of understanding stung like a scratch. And even more so because it wasn't true.

As she had promised, Ratha called the gathering on the following day just before sunset. The Named came to sit before the sunning rock in the old pasture, while the Firekeepers and their leader kindled the meeting fire from torches brought from the fire-den. Ratha noticed that the blaze was made large enough to serve as a beacon to those still coming in from distant corners of clan territory, but not so fierce as to serve as a hypnotic center for the gathering. That way lay danger, as she and Fessran had both learned. Their experience with Shongshar and his fire-worship had taught them caution.

From the sunning rock, she looked down at her friend. Fessran stood to one side, sitting stiffly with a torch in her jaws, shadows dancing across her sand-colored fur. Though at first Fessran had been reluctant, she now allowed and encouraged her Firekeepers to make use of treeling skills. And the treelings had proven more useful to the Firekeepers than anyone could have foreseen. Only this morning, Fessran's assistant, Bira, had showed Ratha a young student who had taught his treeling to twist grass and bark into a long tail strong enough to wrap about a bundle of sticks. With twigs bound together, a Firekeeper could drag much heavier loads.

Ratha had been intending to send the youngster and his treeling out on the search, but now, she decided, she would keep him here and have him teach his new art to others who might use it. The young male would be disappointed at being denied the adventure, but he would be proud to know he had developed a skill worth keeping.

She sat up and spoke of the purpose for this gathering and of the searchers she was sending out to seek new sources of game, pasturage, and water. She was careful to say she would choose only those who could be spared from their duties, so as not to leave the herds vulnerable or the fires unguarded. And when she had finished, she called Thakur and let him take the place of his choosing, facing into the setting sun.

The other searchers, chosen from among both herders and Firekeepers, stood in pairs with their whiskers facing outward. Thakur stood alone. He was used to being by himself with just Aree for company, and he was experienced in fending for himself away from the clan.

"You who will journey have been first to eat from the kill," said Ratha. "Your bellies are full, your legs strong, and the hope of the Named goes with you."

At her word, the scouts started on their search. Thakur glanced back as he took his first steps from the sunning rock. The glow in his eyes and the sheen on his fur told her of his eagerness. The treeling on his back fluffed her fur petulantly, as if saying she was getting too settled for traveling, but she gave her tail a jaunty wave in parting.

Ratha watched the scouts as they left, but her gaze lingered longest on one copper coat.

Though you are not taking the Red Tongue itself, Thakur, she thought, *may the power of its spirit guard you.*

CHAPTER 3

NEWT'S EARS SWIVELED forward as she woke, crawled from her sandstone cave, and limped onto the beach. Her pricked foot was tender but no longer painful, and she soon forgot about it. She tested the wind, finding the smells of creatures she had already encountered, such as the short-tusked walrus, but there was an unfamiliar scent among them. Through the background of wind and waves, she heard a distant clamor with odd hooting sounds breaking through.

Warily she hunched down in the sand, all senses extended for danger. She wondered if she should retreat from the beach and was surprised by a possessive anger that welled up inside her. No. This was her place. She had claimed it, left her footprints here, laid down her scent.

She circled downwind, guided by the strange smell.

It had a strong seaweed-and-fish tang, resembling the scent of the blubber-tusker, but it differed enough from that animal's smell for her to identify it as new. Peering up the beach, she saw a natural jetty of gray sandstone thrusting out to sea beneath a cliff. On the promontory, gray and black shapes sprawled in the sun.

At first she thought these animals resembled the blubber-tusker, but their broad bodies were less blubbery and more compact, slate colored on top and cream below. Chunky fore- and hindlimbs folded back against sleek sides as the creatures lay on their bellies. Their heads were long and tapered, reminding Newt of the muzzle of a forest dappleback rather than the snout of a blubber-tusker. They also had leaf-shaped ears that swiveled and twitched.

Newt narrowed her eyes against the morning sea glare. She felt the sun heat her back while her shadow inched along the sand. The wind gusted, bringing her the briny food-scent of shellfish. She remembered how she had plundered the blubber-tusker's leavings.

As she came around the foot of the steep bluff, she saw a small cove that was sheltered from the wind by sandstone cliffs jutting up on either side. Within that refuge she saw another sea-beast and two smaller companions that resembled it. The large beast wallowed in the surf, while the small ones lay higher on the beach. Newt hid behind the rocks and crept closer for a better look.

The animal lifted its head and pricked its ears, then settled back complacently, chin resting on a short, fat neck. It grunted to itself as the waves washed its sides. Again Newt saw the elongated muzzle, resembling that of a dappleback, but instead of a rounded nose and chin, the creature had a tapered snout with a pronounced overbite. It yawned, revealing downward-pointing incisors in the upper jaw and a cluster of tusks thrusting from the lower.

The sight made Newt uneasy and she hid, but soon the sound of splashing coaxed her to peer out again from her hiding place. The glistening form of the sea-beast slapped against wet sand. With splay-toed webbed forefeet, the creature hauled itself onto the beach, jaws wedged wide open by a huge, muck-covered shell.

The beast seemed to ignore its hind legs, letting them drag behind while it humped and heaved along on belly and stout forelegs. As it crushed the clamshell in its jaws, seawater spurted from the clam's leathery siphon.

Waves of tantalizing scent reached Newt. She licked her chops but forced herself to remain still, waiting. She listened to the scraping and grinding sounds while the shellfish smell made her drool.

The small sea-beasts wiggled on their bellies in the sand. They lurched up on thick legs and bumbled around until they fell against each other or the big one. From the forbearance the large beast showed the two, Newt sensed she was looking at a female and her young.

Newt marked the youngsters as prey, for they were small enough to kill easily. She would have to wait until their parent wasn't paying attention. For the present she would settle for clam scraps.

Her hunger was no longer strong enough to blunt her curiosity, for she had eaten from the blubber-tusker's leavings, and she was intrigued with this new creature. Though this beast ate shellfish, lived on the beach, and had tusks, its face, neck, and ears reminded her of a dappleback, and it was those attributes that made the strongest impression on her. Once she had seen a small mare with two spindly foals, and now this memory emerged as an image, coloring her feelings about the sea-beast family. She stared at the strange mare that swam in the sea.

This creature, whom Newt now thought of as a "sea-mare," continued to wrench apart a huge shell with fore-feet and tusks. The seamare's black forepaws, with their wide tapering toes and the webbing between, were nothing like the flippers of the blubber-tusker or the hoofed toes of a dappleback.

The longer she watched the seamare, the more Newt focused on those odd, splay-toed feet. As she had once identified with an image of herself as the newt, so she identified the seamare with the image of those strange feet. To her, the creature became Splayfoot.

Newt stayed hidden until the seamare finished gorging on clams and fell asleep on a low sandstone shelf, with both seafoals sprawled nearby. Newt smelled a few savory bits remaining from the seamare's feast of shellfish. Carefully she hobbled from her hideaway down through the rocks to the terrace where Splayfoot lay. She got so close she could smell the salty beast-scent and hear the seamare's rumbling snore. Quickly she snatched up the nearest morsel and went for the next.

Suddenly the seamare's neck muscles tightened as the beast lifted her head, her tapered muzzle pointing at Newt. With an ungainly heave, the beast swept both chunky forelegs around and heaved up her forequarters.

From her open mouth came a booming roar that echoed between the rocks of the cove and made Newt skitter back with flattened ears.

For an instant the two confronted each other. With surprising speed, Splayfoot humped herself toward Newt, swinging her tusks. The seamare's anger propelled her up onto her rear legs, and Newt discovered that they weren't as useless as they had first appeared.

Newt hadn't expected the seamare's sudden transformation from belly-dragger to walker. Splayfoot had a clumsy gait, with out-thrust elbows and turned-in feet, but it served well enough. Now the seamare was a four-footed behemoth lumbering toward the enemy that threatened herself and her young.

With a mouth full of sandy clamshells and meat, Newt couldn't use her teeth, but she wasn't about to drop her takings. Gathering her hind feet beneath her, she leaped as high as she could, clinging and scrabbling at the rocks above.

Once she had gained a secure perch, she started to eat, looking down at the seamare. Unable to hold the shell down with both forepaws, she wedged one side of it under a boulder and held it there with her good leg while she worried the meat away with her side teeth.

Splayfoot strained her head back as far as her thick neck would allow and gave a bellow that almost made Newt choke on the rubbery clam flesh she was gulping. The agile youngsters scrambled back to their mother's side as the seamare pointed her muzzle in the air and sniffed suspiciously. Splayfoot lumbered along on her belly, probing the way ahead with the long bristles on her muzzle and stabbing the sand with her tusks, as if she thought the menace might still be lurking there.

She snuffled among the scattered shells, putting back her ears and rolling her eyes. But instead of retreating from the place, as prey animals would when they caught the smell of meat eaters, the seamare gave a bubbling roar and knocked all the remaining shell fragments away with a powerful sweep of her foreleg. She opened her jaws and waggled her head, giving the lurking meat eater a good look at her tusks and teeth.

Newt decided that she'd had her fill of clam scraps. She smelled other things that might be edible, such as carrion and seabird eggs. But first she wanted to rest. She retreated as fast as she could limp back to her refuge at the foot of the weathered sandstone cliff.

Several days later, Newt was picking her way back down through the rocks after a successful egg-hunting expedition. As she licked yolk from her muzzle and turned toward her cave, she heard barks and growls, followed by the seamare's bellow.

On the beach in the cove below, she saw Splayfoot with her two seafoals huddling at her sides. Five small animals with sleek, wet pelts and sinuous shapes surrounded and menaced the family. These small sea lions reminded Newt of the otters she had seen in the ocean, lolling in wave troughs. The otters swam with webbed toes and long, powerful tails, whereas these animals had clawed flippers and much shorter tails. Their ears were small and lay close to their heads, and their eyes bulged. Their muzzles were tapered, with powerful jaws and teeth.

Their bark was hoarse and throaty, unlike the cry of any creature she knew. Both forelimbs were short, the forefeet joining almost directly to the shoulder to form front flippers. The two rear feet lay so far back on the body that they suggested a fishlike tail, but the creatures could bound along at surprising speed by arching their backs. Newt wrinkled her nose at the fishy undertone in their smell.

Splayfoot heaved herself up on her hind legs with bubbling roars and honks, swinging her head with its armament of forward-thrusting tusks. The attackers answered with barks and yelps while they wove about their prey.

Newt felt a growl rumbling in her own throat. She had prowled among these rocks and terraces enough to think of them as her territory. For an instant the growling and barking made her hesitate. A creature bold enough to attack Splayfoot might well prove a threat to her. This made her snarl and put back her ears, rage washing away fear.

Newt sprang down from the terrace and skidded onto the beach in a spray of wet sand. A sleek form slithered at her and struck like a snake, driving its teeth into a rear foot. Yowling, she leaped, twisting herself to pounce backward. One paw landed on the beast, but one wasn't enough. Newt's opponent bared its teeth and barked at her with a blast of fishy breath, then scooted free to bite her on the tail.

Another barking raider grew bold and rushed Splayfoot in a series of bounding jumps. The seamare swung one leg in a clumsy blow that knocked the beast over. As the animal rolled, its forelimbs flapped in the air. In a bound,

Newt was among the pack, lunging on one forefoot and challenging gaping jaws with a snarl.

She found out quickly that the enemies looked clumsier than they were. They dodged her raking kicks and worried her hocks, writhing around and underneath her. She seized one attacker by its thick scruff and threw it aside. Another, trying to tear her crippled foreleg, was met with a hind-foot kick full of open claws that left it squealing and bleeding, but still willing to fight. Newt found herself close to Splayfoot as the seamare clubbed the sleek forms that darted at her from under and around the rocks.

The larger seafoal jabbed out with its small, sharp tusks, while the smaller one clung to its mother's flank. Splayfoot wheeled abruptly to fend off attack from the side, leaving the smaller seafoal unguarded. Bullet heads with large, bulging eyes turned toward it. Three sets of jaws seized its legs. The raiders hopped and scampered backward, dragging the bawling seafoal.

Splayfoot clumped after them, honking her rage as the creatures yanked the seafoal over the jagged rocks, battering its body as they went. By the time they dragged it into the surf, the foal no longer struggled or cried out. Newt saw the seamare halt, show her tusks at the killers, and then swing around to defend her remaining youngster.

Two raiders now remained, the one Newt had tossed aside and another. Newt cut off their charge toward the seamare and seafoal, driving them back. One raider hesitated; the other recklessly attacked Newt's flank. In the heat of the fight, it had forgotten Splayfoot.

The seamare was on it like an angry, rolling boulder, gouging and trampling. With a powerful clout from a forelimb, she belted the raider into the jagged rocks and broke its back. Still twitching, the body slid until it was caught by a spike of rock, where it hung like a stranded mass of sea kelp.

The last raider's barks turned into frenzied yelps. It bounded toward the surf with Newt and Splayfoot after it. In a few steps Newt had outdistanced the seamare, and the chase was all hers.

Too angry to stop herself, Newt galloped into the ocean after the escaping enemy. She slapped and swatted at the sleek, brown form as it bobbed before her on the back of a rolling breaker. She tried to lunge but was thrown off balance by the current and the sand drawing away from beneath her feet. With a wriggle of its glistening body, the enemy disappeared.

Scrambling wildly to keep her footing, Newt fell face first into the next wave. The swirling water pulled her down and spun her around in a gritty whirlpool of brine mixed with sand. It banged her against rocks on the bottom and spewed her up again. Choking on seawater and panic, she paddled on the back of another wave as it lifted her up, dropped her, and sucked her under once again.

She had no idea that moving water possessed such power. River and stream currents tugged at her belly and limbs when she crossed, but these waves tossed her around, playing with her as she would toy with small prey.

Panic ran through her, drumming loudly in her ears.

It became the sound of the Dreambiter's feet behind her, compressing her vision to a narrow tunnel, through which she saw the swirling water as if from a distance. Now the image of the Dreambiter mixed with the surging ocean, but the bite, when it came, was as painful as ever, and the shock made her stop struggling. The currents became claws, pulling her under, and the sound of the waves a triumphant hissing, saying that the Dreambiter had won.

Rage suddenly punched through her growing stupor. She coughed explosively with the air remaining in her lungs, then thrashed with legs and tail against the undertow until her head broke the surface. Gulping air, she felt the frenzy of panic die away and with it the Dreambiter. Her vision opened again; the drumming in her head faded.

With a savage twist, she righted herself, pointed her nose toward the beach, and paddled. In the short intervals between fighting breakers, she noticed something that she hadn't had time to realize: She was stroking with her crippled foreleg. She could feel the unused muscles pull painfully as her limb strove to answer the demands made of it.

Abruptly, a downward stroke of her good forepaw scraped sand. She swung her hind feet down, gained purchase, and pushed hard to climb ashore. The drop-off was steeper than she had expected, but soon the surging water had fallen to her breast, then below her belly. She staggered up the beach, out of the surf, trembling with exhaustion. Her bad foreleg throbbed, but from the ache she gained understanding. If she were forced to use the leg, it would respond. Though its motion was crabbed and constricted by shrunken muscles, the leg would move.

With brine streaming from her coat, Newt limped up the beach, the crippled foreleg tucked against her chest. She was so accustomed to getting around on three legs that the discovery that it would move slipped from her mind.

The episode with the flipper-footed enemies disgruntled her. They escaped her so easily by diving into the ocean. She wanted to master this powerful, surging, rolling water that seemed so much like a living creature. And once she had learned to swim in it, what a surprise she would give those raiders if they attacked again!

A soft thump drew her attention to the body of the one that Splayfoot had killed. It had fallen in a tumbled heap from the rock that had caught it to the sand below. She went to the carcass and nosed it until the body lay on its side.

A grunt made her look up. Splayfoot hunkered a short distance from the carcass, with her seafoal at her flank. Turning her head from side to side, she eyed the dead animal. Newt started to withdraw, afraid that Splayfoot might claim the kill, since she had made it. If the seamares ate clams, they might eat flesh as well. But the seamare satisfied herself with only a few half-hearted pokes, then turned away.

Newt needed no further encouragement. Growling possessively, she seized the prey, sank her teeth deep into its neck, and scuttled off to her cave.

During the next few days, Newt stayed near Splayfoot and her foal. The seamare chased her off only when she ventured too close to the youngster and gradually allowed her to come closer. Splayfoot dredged shellfish from the shoals and brought her catch back to the terrace, where she ate in her usual messy fashion, leaving scraps for Newt to filch.

Splayfoot often left her isolated beach to join with others of her kind, who formed a loosely associated herd. Gradually Newt began to follow her. At first her presence made the herd restless, but soon they became used to her.

After loss of her smaller foal, the seamare lavished all her attention on the larger one. Some of this seemed to spill over toward Newt, who wondered if the seamare was deliberately leaving scraps within easy reach, as if to encourage her.

She made the most of the opportunities Splayfoot gave her, but without thought of gratitude. As she limped back to her cave with a mouthful of clam scraps, she even considered how to distract the seamare and take the surviving seafoal. But that idea soon faded from her mind. Splayfoot and her seafoal became neighbors rather than prey. Without competition from a sibling, the large seafoal could nurse as much as he wanted. Whenever Newt thought of him, she remembered how greedily he guzzled his mother's milk. As the seamare had become Splayfoot to her, so the seafoal became Guzzler.

Having nearly drowned in the rough surf, Newt was fearful of venturing into it again. But she hungered for revenge against the barking raiders who had attacked Splayfoot and then escaped into the ocean.

Several days after the incident, Newt's fear had faded enough to let her try wading in the sea. She chose a long, shallow slope where the waves broke before they rolled in. With her tail flipping apprehensively, she limped into the ocean until the surge came up to her belly. But even gentled surf had currents that tugged at her legs and threatened to unbalance her. The undertow stole the sand from beneath her pawpads, making her feet slide and twist.

As if to demonstrate that there was nothing to make a fuss about, Splayfoot humped herself to the waterline, slipped in, and stood up, the sea helping to buoy her and take the weight off her rear legs. Her stout forelimbs, however, remained firmly planted, unaffected by the strong currents that threatened to wrench Newt's legs out from under her. Newt had already noticed that the seamare's front legs were rigid from elbow to foot, allowing no twisting of the lower leg. This resulted in her clumsy land gait. In the surging currents of the shallows inshore, it became an advantage, for Splayfoot's stout forepaws could not turn beneath her.

Newt staggered on three legs, struggling to keep herself upright. At last she gave up and hobbled up the cove beach above the surf line. The water was too rough. Her ears twitched back with irritation as she watched the seamare cavorting in the breakers. She turned her back on the sea and went foraging.

After satisfying her hunger on seabird eggs, she did not return to her usual sleeping place for a nap but wandered south. Her way led onto the large crescent beach that lay between the seamare's natural jetty and another point to the south. She paced through the crusty sand of the backshore, guided by a dim recollection of the territory she had crossed to come here. Though she did not know what she was looking for, she kept on until she stood atop a low bluff, looking down onto a wide, shallow lagoon.

Unlike the green foamy surf of the jetty, the water here was so clear that she could see tiny wave ripples in the sand at the bottom. It lapped gently against the shore, sheltered from the wind that lashed the open ocean. She came to the water's edge and let it wash the toes of her good forefoot while the intricate lacing of sunlight on the wavelets dazzled her. She waded in, feeling the water seep through her fur. Here in the shallows, it was warmed by the sun and felt tepid instead of cold.

Enjoying the silken stroking of the water against her skin as she moved, Newt waded deeper, letting herself be floated off her feet. She started to paddle, but the splashing was awkward and she stopped. It felt so easy and relaxing to just hang in the water with legs extended, letting herself be teased along by vagrant currents. She wasn't afraid. It was so shallow that she could put her feet down and stop drifting any time she wanted. The noon sun above cast her shadow along the bottom, surrounding it with bright, shimmering rings.

So fascinated was she by this that she ducked her head under to get a better look and got a noseful of brine. A spark of alarm and the memory of her near drowning almost made her panic, but she remembered how a blast of exhaled breath had blown the water out and kept her from choking.

She'd done enough, at least for one day. She hauled herself out, dripping, shook off, and went about her business. She had found what she wanted: a place where she could immerse herself in this strange new element and teach herself to master it.

She began to look forward to her daily jaunts to the lagoon for a swim. This way of moving in water allowed her to use her crippled foreleg much more than when walking. As she stroked with the good forepaw, the backwash swirled around the other, gently tugging and stretching stiffened joints and muscles. Often the leg ached when she limped ashore, but she sensed it was a good hurt and one that might lead to healing.

Her fascination with the patterns of light and shadow cast by the sun on the lagoon bottom led her to try ducking her head under again and opening her eyes. Finding that she could keep water out of her nose and mouth by holding air in her lungs, she could soon submerge her head without feeling suffocated. Her sight underwater was blurry but good enough to let her make out objects on the sandy bottom.

Before long, she abandoned her instinctive but ineffective paddling with her head held above water. Now she stretched out her entire body and immersed her head. She discovered that she could pull herself through the water with sweeping strokes of her good forepaw. Though this worked, she had a tendency to veer off to one side, which she countered by using her bad leg as much as she could.

Though she worked hard to gain skill, she often let herself relax by gliding around in the lagoon, feeling the water caress her belly fur and watching sandy shoals pass beneath. It brought a soothing escape from the demands of her life and the painful memories that still lay like a cloud over her mind. Drifting in liquid silence, she was not reminded of her limitations, either of mind or body. Here the water gave only its gentlest challenge, rewarding her with something rare in her life: pleasure.

Though Newt remained wary of the tailed sea lions that had attacked the seamare's young, she had no idea that a bird might try to take a seafoal. At first she didn't look up from her early morning prowling when the raptor's shadow crossed her path. She often saw sea eagles among the birds overhead, but they had never proved a threat.

The whistling of air through feathers made her stare skyward as a huge black-and-white-crested sea eagle dived at the seamare. It dropped swiftly toward Splayfoot's surviving seafoal, Guzzler, who was sleeping apart from his mother in a sun-warmed hollow of rock. A feeling of guardianship and responsibility as well as the urge to defend her territory sent Newt sprinting to meet the diving bird. The power of her hindquarters drove her so hard and fast that her good foreleg nearly collapsed under the strain.

She charged straight into the mass of feathers and flapping pinions that filled her vision. Talons struck down at Guzzler, but Newt hit first. Leaping high with her good foreleg stiffly extended, she punched the big bird out of the air. The crested eagle flopped to one side, beating its great wings and screaming its wrath. It righted itself on its curved talons and mantled its wings at Newt, turning its head quickly from side to side as if assessing this new threat.

With a defiant scream, it hopped toward the squirming

seafoal. Newt dug her nose under Guzzler, shoved him up and over a lip of rock to get him quickly out of the way.

Lowering her head and hunching her shoulders, she stalked toward the raptor, feeling her frustrations bubble up into a gleeful rage.

With a flap that sounded like a crack, the sea eagle spread its huge, white-tipped wings, startling Newt. Behind her, Splayfoot trumpeted indignantly, but the noise faltered, as if the seamare were having second thoughts about tackling such an unfamiliar enemy as this. Newt couldn't spare a glance at the seamare; the bird flattened its feathered crest and hopped at her, beak open and hissing.

Without a free forepaw to clout the bird, Newt was at a disadvantage. As if it sensed this, the eagle sidled toward its foe. Newt remembered how she had knocked it from the air, centered her weight on her rear legs, and launched herself. Again she hit the big bird, raking loose a cluster of black feathers from its breast. Its beak sliced down, grazing the side of Newt's head. Dancing on her hind legs, Newt made a wide slap with her good paw that connected with the sea eagle's neck. It returned a bruising blow with one wing, then lurched around and tumbled into a flopping, flapping run that finally lifted it off the beach. Gaining altitude over the heads of the seamares, the beaten raptor made one last overhead circle, raining excrement on Newt.

She shook herself, snarled at the retreating bird, then turned, panting, to face Splayfoot. There was a certain spark in the seamare's eyes that made Newt fear the seamare's protective anger over the threat to Guzzler might spill over onto her. She saw Splayfoot make a sudden movement, as if she were about to charge, but something in her eyes changed, and she only grunted and tilted her head to one side, uncertain. Then she swung around and left with Guzzler.

So intent was Newt on Splayfoot that she neither saw nor smelled the stranger who had crept up on the bluff above and crouched, watching.

CHAPTER 4

THAKUR'S WAY of reckoning direction by the sun held true and brought him to the shore he'd seen only from a distant peak. Taking Aree on the journey slowed him down, but he wasn't going to part with his treeling, even for this. Although he had eaten enough at the clan kill to sustain him for several days, he made stops to hone his hunting skills, long left unused by his life in the clan. He also halted to sleep, relieve himself, or let Aree forage for berries and beetles.

They reached the sea coast just before sunset several days after departing from the sunning rock. Thakur had begun to think he had gone astray, for the way led him through a forest of great pines whose fibrous red bark and enormous girth were new to him. But when he kept to the deer trail that wound through these hills and brush canyons, the redwood forest gave way to a lighter growth of strong-smelling bay laurel. It ended abruptly at a meadow.

The grass was high and whipped by a salty breeze. Walking slowly, Thakur left the trees, turning his head to catch the sights, smells, and sounds of this new country. Ahead he heard the muffled crash and sigh of breaking waves. The sound reminded him of some great creature breathing. A bird sailed above him, its underside a dazzling white against the dark-blue sky, its wings constantly shifting to ride the wind that sent it slipping sideways. As the gull winged overhead, Thakur felt Aree flatten against his neck. With a quick nuzzle, he reassured the treeling.

He walked until the wind was strong in his face and the grass thinning beneath his feet. The meadow ended, tumbling away into sheer cliffs with waves pounding at their base. At first, Thakur thought he should taste the water, but night was coming and he could see no way to climb down. Thakur looked down into the frothing surf until he grew dizzy, then gazed outward.

Before him lay a shimmering expanse of silver, where the setting sun's light danced in colors like light from the Red Tongue. At first it appeared to be another land, a vast plain spreading toward the horizon with sunlight painting new trails to lead him onward. The shimmer became the ripple of water, of traveling wave crests that swept toward him.

The first time he'd seen this great water from a distance, he had thought it must be an enormous lake. But now, standing on the cliff and sweeping the horizon for some glimpse of a distant shore, he sensed that even if he journeyed for a lifetime, he would never be able to travel around it. Many a closed circle of pawprints had he left about the lakes near his home ground, but a circle of pawprints about this expanse of water would always remain open.

He gazed out over the water, watching its hues and texture change with the sinking sun. He felt the same awe that touched him when he sat gazing into the heart of a flame. Both were things he knew he would never understand, but he sensed they came from the same source and had the same underlying power. It was a feeling that made him want to stay quiet while evening came to this new and almost sacred place. Even Aree remained still, containing her usual tendency to fidget.

At last the feeling faded into simple loneliness, and the wind began to bite. Thakur got up from the place where he had settled and stretched himself. He padded back through the grass to the edge of the forest and found shelter in a niche between two logs that had fallen across each other. There he and the treeling passed the night.

When Thakur awoke at dawn, the sound of breakers was fresh in his ears and the sunlight brilliant. The shoreline country now had an exuberant quality that infected both travelers. Frolicking and scratching with energy, Aree pounced aboard Thakur's back, and they set off.

With a flick of his tail, he turned from the westward path he'd been on to a northward course that led him up the coast. He hoped to find a way down to the water's edge, but the cliffs remained too forbidding. He trotted along windblown scarps with Aree munching berries and dribbling the juice on his fur. He crossed wild clifftop meadows and paced over the flanks of hills whose slopes were cut off by the sheer drop of the sea cliffs. He paused to rest in groves of coast pine where the trees leaned the way of the prevailing wind, their shapes stunted and twisted by spray and storm.

The variety and abundance of birds amazed him. They wheeled about him in raucous flocks or glided silently overhead. Fork-tails hovered in midair by beating their pointed wings into a blur and shifting their tails to balance the wind. Sea gulls swooped so low over him that he had to fight his instinct to spring up and bat one out of the air. Though he forced himself to ignore the birds, his tail twitched, and he could not keep his teeth from chattering in excitement as he trotted along.

By midday the stark cliffs had given way to friendlier country that hosted river valleys and winding estuaries. As Thakur descended with Aree from the clifftops, he saw sandy shores and mudflats. Droves of stilt-legged shorebirds rested or waded there, probing the bottom with their bills.

Some of these birds were so odd that he halted to gaze at them. He knew the long, sharp bills of herons and the broad ones of ducks, but here he saw beaks that curved up, down, or even sideways.

The shorebirds looked so clumsy and gawky that he was tempted to stalk one. But Aree would be in the way, and there was no convenient tree where she could wait safely until he had finished his hunt.

At one estuary, there was a place that looked shallow enough to ford. There he tried the water, but gagged at the briny taste. Disappointed, he waded across, the current tugging at his legs, while Aree made wordless treeling noises as to what she would do if he got her wet.

Shaking his paws dry on the far side, he found himself behind a line of scrub-covered dunes. He climbed them and stood looking out on a crescent beach that reached to a rocky headland.

He had set one paw into the crusted sand when a swell of noise rose above the soft wailing of the wind. Abruptly he froze, ears swiveling to catch and identify the sound. It was a mixture of animal cries: grunts, bellows, screeches. What made him turn from his intended path was a faint but unmistakable caterwaul that sounded like one of the Named in a squabble.

He listened, his ears strained far forward, his muzzle pointing toward the rocky terraces that formed the promontory north of the beach.

There it was again. Could one of Ratha's scouts have gone astray and ended up here? He doubted it, but he had to make sure. Rather than follow the sweep of the beach, he decided to circle back behind and climb up the bluff, where he could peer down at the rocks and ledges below.

Soon he was trotting through the short grass and scrub brush of the headlands, heading for the point. He could hear more clearly the commotion of the fight going on among the rocks below. Screeching, yowling, and a powerful roar made him quicken his pace, but it was the female voice rising in a battle cry that made his whiskers stand on end.

He broke into a canter, jolting Aree along. Behind an outcropping of sandstone, he slithered to a stop and peered down onto the wave-cut terraces and tumbled rocks that spilled out from the point in a natural jetty.

In a cove along the spit, he saw a female of his own kind facing a huge black-and-white-crested eagle. Nearby was a large web-footed creature. Close to the bird lay a smaller animal that looked like a youngster.

At first he thought the strange female was fighting for her own life against the eagle and readied himself to charge down into the fray. But he saw that the bird hopped toward the small creature every chance it could get, while the female beat it away. When she abruptly turned and nosed the clumsy young animal over a lip of rock and out of the bird's reach, Thakur realized this was no simple conflict of hunter and hunted. This stranger, whoever she was, fought to defend the young of the sea-beast just as Named herders protected dappleback foals and three-horn fawns.

Abruptly the fight ended. With a great clapping of wings, the bird lifted and flapped away. Thakur peered hard at the stranger, trying to see if she were clan-born or one of the more intelligent among the Un-Named, but he failed.

Her rust-black and orange coloration was unlike anything he had seen before. She seemed to be limping. He thought at first that the bird had wounded her, but as he studied her closely, he realized her three-legged walk was habitual, and he guessed that the drawn-up foreleg must be permanently lame.

Thakur wondered if what he'd seen was only his imagination. Could it be that his training as a herder and his work as a teacher made him misinterpret the stranger's behavior? Was he seeing only what he expected to see? Well, he could hardly have expected this! He watched the stranger wend her way among the odd, lumpy sea-creatures, their calmness convincing him that they knew her and had grown accustomed to her presence.

The stranger's smell was faint at this distance, but the trace of it he could catch was not clan scent. Curious now, he cast about until he found a scent-mark she had made on the bluff and inhaled the odor. No, she wasn't from the clan, nor was she of the Un-Named, who left their traces on hunting trails.

Thakur toyed with the idea of going down to meet this intriguing stranger, but something made him hesitate.

She must be from the fringes of the Un-Named, he decided, a product of a mating between a clan member and one of the Un-Named, just as he and his brother, Bonechewer, were. If so, she might be friendly, but she also might be dangerous. Though crippled, she had managed to beat off a bird bigger than she was. Thakur wasn't sure he wanted to confront her directly and certainly not with Aree on his back.

Instead, he watched her, being careful to keep downwind so she wouldn't smell him. He noted the trails she took through the terraces and rocks. If he scent-marked a shrub or boulder along her way, then he could announce himself in a casual fashion and see from a distance what her response would be.

He put his plan into action the following day. After spraying several shrubs and rubbing his chin on a boulder, he sent Aree to safety in the branches of a wind-gnarled cypress and hid himself above the path.

Soon he heard footfalls in the rhythm of his quarry's

three-legged gait. He peered from his hideaway for the first close-up view of the stranger. He was not prepared for the odd little face that appeared around the edge of a boulder. None of the Named had anything like her markings in orange and rusty black. An inky band across the lower part of her face emphasized the lightness of her eyes.

Thakur had never seen such eyes. An iris of milky green swirled about each slit pupil, giving the stranger a gaze that seemed distracted and diffuse. Yet her stare had an unsettling quality. The cloudiness at first made him think she might be blind, but the sharp definition of her pupils and the way she made her way without using her whiskers to touch things convinced him she could see.

The stranger's ears flicked back, and her neck extended as she caught his scent. He saw her upper lip curl back, revealing short, sharp fangs without signs of wear. She took one limping step toward the bush he had sprayed and then went rigid. A look of terror and rage shot through her eyes. Reeling backward as if she'd been struck, she crumpled into a whimpering heap, her good forepaw shielding her face. Shudders racked her, throwing her on her side, where she fought and thrashed against some unseen enemy.

Thoroughly bewildered, Thakur crept from his hideaway. He had seen and smelled many reactions to his scent-marking, but none as dramatic or frightening as this! An irrational sting of guilt hit him for daring to place his mark in her path.

The young female lay on her side, pedaling weakly

with three feet as she stared ahead. Her head arched back and she stared without seeing. As the paroxysm spent itself, her limbs stilled and her eyes closed. She lay limply. When Thakur pawed her, she wobbled like a freshly killed carcass.

Numbed by astonishment and disbelief, he went to her head and stared down at her. Part of him insisted that it was coincidence; she had sniffed his mark just as the fit struck her. No. He had seen too clearly the shock and fright that had flashed through the cloudiness of her eyes in that instant before she fell.

She took quick, struggling breaths that jerked her rib cage. Thakur himself took a sharp breath of relief. As her breathing steadied, he felt his panic drain away. Whatever the cause of this attack, it would run its course. Unable to sit still, he paced around her.

The stranger's face resembled those of the Named. She had a delicate muzzle and a well-defined break from the line of nose to forehead that Thakur found attractive. But what made him start when he saw it was a line of reddish-tan flame that licked up her forehead from the top line of her eyes to the crown of her head. Against the background color of rusty black, the strange marking stood out. It seemed to waver and flicker in his gaze, as if he were looking once again at a windblown line of fire. In his memory, the Red Tongue made its march through the forest.

Suddenly Thakur felt angry with himself. Yes, she had strange markings, but there was nothing that should disturb him about the patterns on her face. There were little touches of white at the corners of her lips and a narrow cream blaze on her nose. In a Named female, the effect would have been one of disturbing ugliness, or perhaps beauty. . . .

If her smell had matched the unsettling attractiveness of her face, Thakur might have found it harder to break off his close examination of the stranger. But his nose continued to remind him that she was ungroomed, filthy, and so full of the pungent stink of the sea-creatures that he couldn't make out her underlying scent.

She swallowed. The abrupt movement of her throat startled him. Soon she would wake. Should he stay or go? Was it his scent that had thrown her into this fit, and would it happen again if he stayed?

He looked down at her crippled foreleg. Along her shoulder from nape to breast ran a half-collar of rumpled fur that, he guessed, might hide a ridge of scar tissue. The foreleg itself, though shrunken, didn't appear deformed. He had seen a similar injury in a herdbeast, caused when one creature kicked another in the breast. Whatever made the leg move gradually died, until the creature could no longer use its limb. He remembered that herders had soon chosen the animal for culling.

He saw the stranger's eartip tremble. Her lips drew back, exposing her fangs as she swallowed again. He noted the shade of her gums to check if she had lost blood or had the paling sickness. No.

He drew back, then changed his mind. If the fit left her weak or ill, she would need help. But his reason for staying was more than that. What he had seen her doing with the sea-creatures might be valuable to the Named.

At last, after many preliminary stirrings and twitchings, she blinked and moved her head. Thakur sat down where he was, letting her gaze find him. Her nape fur rose, and the pupils of her milky-green eyes shrank. Despite her lame foreleg, she moved so fast that she was a rust-and-black blur in his eyes. In the next instant, she faced him, body displayed broadside, head twisted, fangs bared. The upturned tips of her flattened ears signaled fear as well as anger.

Thakur slowly got to his feet, lifting his tail in the greeting gesture common among the Named. He gave a rising purr.

The other stiffened her defensive posture, her back legs doing an angry little dance of their own that tended to swing her hindquarters toward him. He watched her tail. If it relaxed and curved into a hook, that meant he might have some chance of reaching her.

"I won't hurt you," he said slowly. "Please. I want to talk to you. My name is Thakur."

He faltered on the last word. There was no understanding in those milky-green eyes, not even curiosity. He might as well have tried to speak to a herdbeast! She spat at him and made a pitiful wrenching motion with her stunted foreleg, as if hoping to use it to claw him. He lowered his head and tail. How could this be? How could she have established that unusual relationship with the sea-creatures if she was as dull as this? Herding wasn't a simple task; that he knew well. You had to outthink the creatures you wanted to control; you had to plan ahead.

He stared at her in dismay, his tail sagging. She backed away in a three-legged crab walk, growling deep in her throat.

"Go then," he said sadly, more to himself than to her. Deliberately he broke eye contact, looking away. When he looked back again, she was gone.

Once Thakur had recovered Aree, the treeling cheered him, but he still remained puzzled about his encounter. He walked along the low bluff above the beach with Aree on his back, airing his thoughts aloud to his small companion as he often did.

"She doesn't speak. I'm sure of that," he said over his shoulder to the treeling. "And her eyes are those of a witless Un-Named one." He stopped, remembering the swirling milky-green irises. Were those eyes indeed empty, or did the opacity hide the spark of intelligence that the Named valued? What about her led him to brood this way? *Her companionship with the sea-beasts*, part of him answered, but another, more honest part said *no, that is not all*.

He needed to find forage and a steady supply of good, fresh water for the clan and its herds. He had already noticed several estuaries and inlets that cut into the coastline, but most that he sampled were too salty or brackish, even when he moved upstream. Sparse rainfall had dried up the rivers that fed the bays and inlets, allowing seawater to intrude.

Finally he found a creek that fed a lagoon. Though the lagoon water was briny and mixed with the sea, the stream itself, when he tasted it, was fresh. He followed the creek inland until he came to its source. At the base of a second tier of cliffs set far back from the ocean, a spring ran steadily from a cleft in blue-gray stone, collecting in a pool beneath. Shaded by the rock walls and watered by the spring, trees grew at the base of the cliffs with an open meadow beyond. Seepage from the spring moistened the ground, and fresh grass sprouted amid the dappled patterns of sun and shade.

Here, near the sea coast, morning and evening fogs muted the heat that blistered areas farther inland. Thakur drank from the pool, then stood on its margin, letting the feel of the place seep into him.

Several small pawprints in the moist earth near the pool told him that the stranger too knew of this spring. And seeing her prints made Thakur wonder what would happen if the Named did choose to come. She could always drink from the creek that spilled out of the overflow from the spring-fed pool instead of from the pool itself.

His belly gave a twinge: not true hunger, but a warning that he should eat within the next day or so. His time here was drawing to an end; the other scouts that Ratha had sent out would be returning with descriptions of their discoveries. He too would tell his story to those assembled before the sunning rock. This place, with its oasis of fresh growth and unfailing water, appeared ideal for the clan and their herd animals. In addition, the sea-beasts might be the answer to Ratha's quest for another source of meat. If a lame Un-Named one had formed a protective relationship with one of them, surely the herders of the Named could do more.

Yet even as he thought this he had misgivings. He sensed that the relationship of the stranger to the sea-beasts was different from that of the clan herders to their animals. The creatures' reactions as she walked among them told Thakur that she had blended herself into their community. She lived *with* them rather than managing them to serve her needs, as the Named did with their animals.

But she was alone and weak as well. This was the only way she could live, by disturbing the sea-beasts as little as possible. Perhaps she was only a scavenger after all, he thought, but the idea saddened him.

Could she perhaps find a place among the Named? And if the clan came, with their herds and their ways, could she live a better life than one of scratching and scrounging among middens left by these wave-wallowers?

No. She was not like his people. He doubted if she could accept clan ways even if the Named chose to share them. A promise lay behind her shuttered eyes, but not one the Named could easily trust. Could it be that hers was a different sort of intelligence, one that might show not in mastery of words or brightness of eyes, but in another way?

Thakur knew that he could determine whether that intelligence—that light—would be given a chance to develop or not. If he returned and stood before the sunning rock to say that nothing here would be of value to the Named, this stranger could continue to live her life among the seamares without interference.

He sighed deeply, knowing this path was not open to him. He could not lie to his clan leader or betray his people for the sake of some odd castoff. He would speak, and herders from the clan would come, for the spring-watered trees and meadow offered the Named refuge from the worsening drought. And the wave-wallowing animals might well become an unusual, though successful, addition to the beasts the Named now tended. Their meat might taste a bit odd, but in times of need, the Named couldn't be particular about taste.

He knew where his loyalties lay, and it saddened him. The stranger would be pushed out, tossed aside, and no one would think anything of it because she had no light in her eyes. *But that would be wrong, because we can learn from her. Even if she can't speak, she teaches us by what she does. Ratha must be made to understand.*

With that thought, Thakur got to his feet, coaxed Aree to his shoulder, and set off on his return journey.

Newt spent the rest of that day, after the confrontation with Thakur, hiding in the deepest sandstone hollow she could find. Panic closed around her, making her want to run blindly away from this place and the stranger whose sudden arrival and smell woke the old terrors.

His smell. Her nose had not lied to her. Yes, he had his own scent, but mixed in with it she had caught the hated stink of the Dreambiter. But the Dreambiter was not real, could not leave a true scent except in memory. Newt had thought the Dreambiter's scent was as unreal as the apparition itself, until the newcomer's odor-mark sent its shock through her and brought the nightmare down to rend her. Now she shuddered at the recollection and thought only of fleeing.

But a part of her fought against deserting the beach and the seamares. That she might be forced to abandon this new life she had built for herself was a bitterness she couldn't swallow. Why had he come? What did he want?

She remembered other encounters with those of her kind, of snarls and sneers and the coldness of hate. She had left all that behind. Would she have to return to it once again?

But worst of all was knowing that the newcomer could wake the Dreambiter. Was he the source of the apparition in her dreams that slashed and crippled her? She bared her teeth at the thought but knew that he was not. Though his smell carried enough traces of the Dreambiter's to trigger the onrush of the hallucination, his scent itself was not the cause.

Newt's smell-memories of that maiming attack were stronger than the sight-images. The odor of the one whose teeth had torn her flesh was seared into the center of her being. The smell betrayed one thing: that the Dreambiter was female. Whatever dangers this invading male brought were his own. He might wake her apparition, but he wasn't the source of it.

If she ever found the one who was, she promised herself there would blood and fur scattered until she took the hated one's life in payment for her pain or gave up her own.

She crouched in her cave, thinking about the strange male and shivering. Slowly she realized that he himself had done nothing to threaten or harm her. His voice and his tail gestures were not those of one who wished her ill. His manner was careful, gentle, with a quality she was slowly starting to recognize, for she had known it once long ago.

A picture formed in her mind of the copper-furred, amber-eyed face of the one who had loved her and tried so hard to teach her. And then came an image of the intruder, who also seemed to want her to respond. The two faces were strangely alike, even though one had green eyes and the other amber.

A forgotten part of Newt cried out for more of what she had once known. She wanted kindness and the friendly sound of a purr, the sight of a tail lifted in greeting. When had she heard, felt, and seen those things? So long ago that she could barely remember . . . or was it the mist drifting through her mind that made it all seem so distant?

The Dreambiter had taken it all away.

As Newt lay in her cave, she felt her anger and confusion harden into stubbornness. She would stay here. If she had to face the strange male, she would. The life she was starting to build among the seamares was too precious to yield. No one would drive her away. Not even the Dreambiter.

CHAPTER 5

IN THE LATE-AFTERNOON shade of a thicket on the meadow's edge, Ratha watched a young Fire-keeper and his treeling tangle two cords made from twisted bark. Fessran sat nearby, still without her treeling.

"Tell me again why this would be useful," Ratha said,

trying to understand what Fessran's student was to show her.

"Well, you know that we wrap wood with those lengths of twisted bark so that we can drag more of it. The trouble is that our wrapping often doesn't hold, so the bundle comes apart, the sticks get scattered, and we have to gather them again. When this student showed me a way to prevent that, I decided you should know."

Looking nervously at the clan leader, the young Firekeeper pawed apart the two cords, then began again.

"I don't see any wood, and he's using separate pieces," Ratha objected.

"It's easier to see what he's doing without twigs in the way. And think of the separate bark-twists as the ends of a single one," Fessran soothed.

Ratha gave up arguing and watched. She saw how well the youngster and his small companion worked together, as if each knew what the other needed and expected. He had been born after treelings had become a part of clan life, and the two had been raised together.

She listened to the young Firekeeper and his treeling as the two purred and chirred back and forth, exchanging gestures and nudges. The two strings of bark came together under treeling hands, but both wills worked the change.

Ratha asked them to stop so she could see how the cords wound about each other.

"Think of it this way, clan leader," said the Firekeeper student. "Two snakes have crossed over each other, then the one underneath has looped back and crawled over the top one."

Ratha stared hard. She was beginning to get the idea. *Do you see what he's doing, Ratharee?* she thought at her treeling, who perched on her head, peering down between her ears. *I think I do. Perhaps we can try it together.*

The student pulled his tangled cords apart. Ratharee didn't need any nudging to scramble down from Ratha's back to get her paws on this intriguing new toy, but she had no idea how to repeat what the Firekeeper's treeling had done. With soft prrrups and nudges, Ratha directed Ratharee's hands until the bark cords wound once about each other on the ground.

"Now the wrapped snakes rise up and face each other," said the young Firekeeper, warming to his task, "and they wind again, but they must go in the opposite direction, or the tangle won't hold. We pull both tails, and the snakes tighten about each other," he said as his treeling completed tying the knot.

Ratha had the idea, but getting Ratharee to translate that understanding into action was difficult. She could wind the cords, but she wanted to continue wrapping them about each other until she'd turned them into a tangled mess. However much Ratha nudged, purred, and pawed, she couldn't get past that.

"It isn't easy, clan leader," the student said apologetically. "I had to work a lot with my treeling before we could even do the first part."

"Yes, and I thought you were just fooling around. I cuffed you for not attending to your duties, as you remember well." Fessran grinned as her protégé looked slightly dismayed. She sniffed the treeling-made knot.

"All right, youngster," Fessran announced to the young Firekeeper. "Enough for now. Go back to your work. Since the clan leader likes what you've done, you may continue it, but don't use that as an excuse to be lazy."

Ratha called Ratharee to her and watched the student lope away with his ring-tailed companion on his back.

"He's clever, isn't he? Makes me feel old and stupid." Fessran sighed.

"If you got yourself another treeling, my Firekeeper friend, you could do the same things."

"No. If I can't have Fessree, I'd prefer to burn my whiskers myself. And have smart young students to think up easier ways to bundle wood."

"It may go beyond just wood bundling. You know that, since you're encouraging him," Ratha pointed out.

"It may, but nothing will ever top what a certain young herder did with the Red Tongue." Fessran lay down beside Ratha, pawing her playfully.

"Flatterer! No one will ever accuse you of being old and stupid, not while you have a voice to tease me with. What power has the Red Tongue compared to Fessran's?" With that, Ratha rolled over and play-wrestled with the Firekeeper, while Ratharee scolded both.

The sound of rustling brush and trotting feet brought both heads up. The sun flashed on a dark copper coat as Thakur jogged toward them and slowed to touch noses. With a rising purr, he rubbed past Ratha.

"It is good to smell you again, Thakur," she said softly. "I've thought often of you."

"And I have missed you, yearling. I have much to tell, but first let me rest."

He touched noses with Fessran, then flopped himself down in the shade with Aree on his shoulder.

"I thought everyone would still be off yowling in the bushes," he said, grinning at both of them. "Did you hear any good courting songs this year, Fess?"

The Firekeeper hissed scornfully. "None of this year's crop of suitors has any voice at all."

"So we make cubs by singing? That is something new among the Named." Thakur lolled his tongue at her.

Hearing Thakur's teasing was like old times, but it also served to remind Ratha that the delayed mating season had been short, with few of the Named taking part. Her own heat had lasted only a few days, then tapered off.

Thakur turned to Ratha. "Have the other scouts returned yet?"

"They've been coming in during the past few days. You're the last. Everyone's hungry. I'll have a herdbeast culled."

Thakur's brow furrowed slightly. "The last cull took all the unfit animals. Have the herders choose carefully. We need good stock for breeding."

Ratha felt slightly irritated at him for telling her something she knew well. But he was right; they had to be careful.

"Those who have journeyed far for the sake of their clan shall not sleep tonight with empty bellies," she answered. "We will take what is needed, no more. Fessran, I'd like to speak with Thakur alone. Would you go and look to the culling?"

The Firekeeper sprang to her feet and padded away. Ratha turned to Thakur. "So then, herding teacher. What tales do you bring?"

He paused, then answered. "I have news, but first tell me what the other scouts have reported."

Ratha wondered why he was being evasive, but she said only, "The scouts found many new beasts, but none appear to be as well suited to our needs as the creatures we now keep."

"Oh?" Thakur cocked his head. "That surprises me."

"Young Khushi came back with a wild tale about huge, shaggy creatures who bear tusks and wear their tails on their faces. Although he didn't think we could kill the big ones, he thought we might take the young."

"While their mothers' backs are turned, of course," said Thakur with a grin, for he knew how fiercely protective herdbeast mothers could be.

Ratha glanced at him and went on. "I may go with him to see these face-tails, since we might be able to use them. After all, my grandfather brought us three-horns, and everyone told him they were too dangerous. We just need to learn new ways of managing certain animals."

"Did any other scout find something worthwhile?"

She sighed. "I suppose you didn't find anything either, since you're so eager to know if others did. There were some reports that I considered as possibilities. One scout said he saw many prong-horns. He also spoke of lowing beasts with widespread horns and great humps on their shoulders. He thought the prong-horns too small and fleet for our keeping and the others too ugly tempered. Again, I said I might go with him to judge the creatures for myself." After a pause she noticed he wasn't listening but seemed to be turned inward as if thinking hard. "What's the matter, Thakur?"

Slowly he answered, "Ratha, I did find some creatures on the sea coast that we might herd. They are strange, but they can be managed, and I think I know how."

Carefully he described the seamares, including their shore-dwelling existence. "These water-beasts are larger than our dapplebacks and will provide more meat per cull. They have tusks, but they are clumsy on land."

"These creatures do sound strange, Thakur," Ratha said doubtfully after he had finished. "Fat, tusked dapplebacks with short legs and duck's feet? And you say they swim in this great, wave-filled lake you found? How would we keep one from just swimming away if it didn't want to be our meat?"

"How do we keep our herdbeasts from running away when we cull them? There are ways, especially when we work together."

Ratha stared at her paws. "I suppose. But it sounds as if herding these creatures would cause a big change in the way our herders do things. And it might not work out."

With a sharpness in his voice that betrayed a flicker of injured pride, he said, "Clan leader, I know we can live off these seamares because I have seen another doing it."

Ratha's whiskers bristled and her pupils expanded. She turned her head to stare at him. He looked uncomfortable, as if he had said more than he meant to. "One of our kind?"

"I don't know who she is," Thakur confessed. "She may come from among the fringes of the Un-Named who have bred with the clan. I tried to speak with her, but she doesn't talk. At least not in the way that we do."

He went on to describe the way the young stranger had blended into the seamare colony.

"A small number of us may be able to do the same thing," he said. "Perhaps by watching her, we can learn."

"She actually herds these duck-footed dapplebacks?" Ratha asked. "Are you sure you didn't just see what you wanted to see, herding teacher? She could have been an Un-Named one passing among them. From what you say, she doesn't sound as though she has the light in her eyes or the wit to understand herding."

"I watched her fight off a crested sea eagle from a duck-footed foal. I also saw her swimming with the creatures and sharing their food. Whatever she is doing has a purpose. What's more, the fact she has done it amazes me even more because she's lame." He described how the odd stranger got about on three legs, keeping one forepaw tucked against her chest.

Ratha eyed him. "You seem to have been taken with this bit of an Un-Named one."

"Do you think I missed the mating season so much that I would consider taking an outside female?" Thakur flashed his teeth at her in irritation. "You and I, of any among the Named, should know the dangers of that!"

"I don't seem to have to worry," Ratha said, her voice turning bitter. "I know I won't have cubs this year, even though the courting fever took me as it did the others. Perhaps it is better that I don't, since I have all of the clan to look after." She laid her nose on her paw for a minute and stared ahead into nothing. "I'm sorry, herding teacher. I didn't mean that. Words can hurt more than claws sometimes."

"Well, in any case, I wasn't tempted," Thakur said, still ruffled. "She wasn't in heat. She also stank of wave-wallower dung and fish."

Ratha pensively licked the back of a forepaw. She glanced at him from the corner of one eye. "I will come with you to the lake-of-waves, and you can show me these animals. But you'll have to wait for a few days. We're driving the beasts to another river tomorrow."

"I was afraid you'd have to do that soon," Thakur said. "So the nearby one has gone dry."

"And I don't know how long this new one can supply us."

"Well, another good reason for going to see those duck-footed dapplebacks is that I found a spring near their beach." He went on to describe the gush of water from the face of a shaded cliff so well that Ratha became uncomfortably aware of her dry tongue. The drought was progressing so rapidly that a reliable water source had become more important than new game animals.

"I'm interested in the spring," Ratha said. "I'm thinking of moving our animals permanently to another place until this drought ends."

Abruptly Thakur asked, "Will you need me on the next drive? If you would allow me to get a head start on the journey back to the lake-of-waves, I could take another look at the spring. It would also help me learn more about the creatures there."

"And the odd one who lives among them."

Thakur rolled onto his chest, his front paws spread out before him. "She has much to teach me, I think. Suppose you lead the first drive until the herders can manage alone. Then you and Fessran join me on the shore."

"By ourselves?"

"Yes."

"Why not bring others who are not needed to manage our own animals?"

"I'm afraid too many of us would scare our little sea-dappleback herder away. Let me go first, then the two of you. She might get used to me. Perhaps she can talk but was just too frightened."

"Are you thinking of trying to bring her into the clan if she can speak?" Ratha asked. She knew Thakur could hear the wary edge in her voice. He too remembered what had happened when she had admitted an unknown stranger to the ranks of the Named.

"Let us run that trail when we find it," said Thakur smoothly. "First I want to learn from her. If the question of clan admittance arises, you, as leader, will have to decide. I don't think it's going to be a problem. If she can't speak, how is she going to ask?" He crossed one paw over the other, the gesture ending his words.

"Well, she doesn't sound as though she will be too clever for her own good, as Shongshar was," Ratha growled. "All right, herding teacher. Your plan sounds like a good one."

"Then I will leave again after I've eaten and rested," he answered. "When you are ready, follow me." He then told her the way to the shore and said he would leave scent-marks to guide her. He asked her to leave her own signs, once she got there, to tell him she'd arrived. She listened carefully, remembering his words.

Ratha got up as she spotted Fessran's tan form jogging back toward her.

She turned to Thakur. "Hungry?"

She didn't need an answer as the herding teacher scrambled to his feet, his belly growling.

Several days later, the Named and their herds were treading the way to another river that lay farther from clan ground. Dust swirled, kicked up by the feet of the lead three-horns. Ratha kept her eye on the gray-coated stag and the two herders to either side of him. If the Named could keep him moving steadily, the others would follow. They had gotten him away from the trickling remains of the first river after several attempts that nearly became fights. She thought she might have to order the stag culled, but that would cause the loss of a good sire and throw the herd into disarray.

She had delayed the decision to move their watering site as long as possible, but when the sluggish trickle in the river became stagnant and she found three-horns pawing the streambed to find water that wasn't scummy or thick with mud, she knew they had to make the trek. It hadn't been easy to get the animals organized and the herders ready. She glanced at the lead stag again.

Though the beast was cooperating now, a certain look in his eye, and the way he tossed his head, made Ratha wary. The two herders looked nervous, switching their tails with every step. They were strong but still young. How she wished she had brought Thakur after all, but he was far away on his journey to the coast.

Ratha decided to bring another herder up, just in case the three-horn became obstinate. Khushi. He was a good one. From a timid cub, he had grown into a steady, patient young herder who understood three-horns, although lately he had been showing a tendency to disappear when someone wasn't with him. Ratha decided she needed to give him a reminder about clan responsibilities. Odd, though—he wasn't one she would describe as lazy.

She trotted back along the line of beasts and herders, sneezing dust from her nose. Her tongue felt leathery against her teeth, and she couldn't help thinking of the rainy season, when the brook ran full and lively through the pastures.

Firekeepers flanked the main three-horn herd. They walked in guard positions, some carrying torches bearing the Red Tongue. Bright sun and blowing dust diminished the fire's light, making it look pale against the sky.

Ratha searched for Khushi, calling out his name against the bawling and rumbling of the herd. She searched the throng of animals and herders without finding him, gave up, and sent another herder. Irritated, she jogged past the outskirts of the flock, intending to scold the errant youngster.

She caught sight of the Firekeeper leader walking near a torchbearer. Khushi was Fessran's son, although the Named tended to forget such things once a cub was grown.

"Where's Khushi?"

The Firekeeper's tail came up in surprise. "How should I know? I don't keep track of him anymore."

"Maybe you should. This isn't the first time I've caught him shirking."

A crackle of brush made Ratha turn her head. Khushi came bounding out from between two low hills. His ears sagged as he slowed his pace.

"Are you still a litterling that I have to insult Fessran

by asking where you are?" she said sharply to him. "You should have been in the lead. The old stag is planning trouble again."

Khushi gulped, lowered his head, and wheeled toward the front, but Ratha stopped him. "You're too late. I've already sent someone. If you don't want to work with three-horns, I'll place you in the rear, with the dappleback herd."

"No, clan leader, it's not that. . . ."

"Well, what is it, then? I'm fed up with looking for you and finding you gone. I'm tempted to put you back with the herding students for some lessons about laziness."

"Wait, Ratha," the Firekeeper interrupted. "He's not usually lazy. There must be some reason."

Khushi sat up and gave his ruff a few strokes with his tongue. He still looked and smelled ashamed, but there was a certain sense of relief, as if he had been carrying a burden and could now let it down.

"Clan leader, you remember that you sent me as a scout to look for game," he began.

"Yes, and you told us about the face-tailed animals," Ratha said.

Khushi took a breath. "After I saw the face-tails, the Firekeeper I was with stumbled across an Un-Named one. It was a female with cubs, and she must have been moving them when we found her."

Ratha waited, wondering what this had to do with his periodic desertion of the herd.

"She was odd looking," Khushi said. "The same gray color as old Shongshar, the same eyes, and the same long teeth."

Ratha felt the hair prickle along her back at the mention of Shongshar's name. She remembered how she and Thakur had left the cubs Shongshar had sired far beyond clan ground. The place she'd chosen offered some limited chances for them to find food. Could it be that one or both cubs had managed to survive and even to have their own young? The gray female Khushi described would be about the right age.

"Shongshar's cubs by Bira?" Fessran was staring at Ratha in open amazement. "But you said they were witless and killed them."

Ratha flinched at Fessran's words. "I didn't kill them; I abandoned them. In a place where they could eat insects and other things."

Fessran took a long breath. "By the Red Tongue's ashes, Ratha, if you'd told me what happened to them, things might have turned out differently with Shongshar."

"Yes, you would have gone out to find the empty-eyed cubs you fostered after Bira left them. That wouldn't have done us much good either," Ratha snapped. "Let Khushi tell the rest of his story."

With a curious glance at Fessran, Khushi went on. "The Un-Named female looked at me in a way that made me shiver and then ran off with a cub in her mouth. But she left one behind and didn't come back for him." Khushi halted, swallowed. "He's over there, beneath the bushes."

Ratha sagged back on her haunches, staring at Khushi in disbelief. "You mean you brought the cub back with you?"

He hung his head. "I'm sorry. It was a stupid thing

to do. But once I'd been near him, his mother wouldn't take him back. I put him out and waited as long as I could, but we'd scared her off for good."

"How did you feed him?" Fessran wanted to know.

"The same way you fed me when you were weaning us from milk to meat. You burped up soft food from your stomach. I had eaten enough from the clan kill before I went scouting that I could do the same."

Ratha started to pace. If the drought and the herd weren't enough to cope with, now she had to deal with a young herder with motherly delusions and an orphaned cub that might well be Shongshar's grandson. She stopped, turned to Khushi.

"If this wild tale is true and not just an elaborate excuse to make me sheath my claws, all I can ask is why didn't you tell me about him?"

Khushi shuffled his paws in the dust. "Well, you were gone just after that, and when you came back, you were busy, and the longer I waited, the harder it got to tell you."

"So you've been sneaking away to feed this Un-Named litterling with food from your own belly."

"And to move him too," Khushi added. "When these river drives started, I thought I'd have to leave him behind, but I found that if I ran really fast with him in my mouth and got ahead of the herd, then I could hide him and then work until the herd passed the hiding place and—"

"All right," Ratha interrupted. "Show me."

Khushi led them away from the line of animals, up over the crest of a hill and down the other side. He jogged to a low bush with peeling red bark and thorny leaves, pulled a dead branch aside, and peered in. A weak mew came from inside. Lying in a hollow between gnarled roots was a tiny, thin, spotted shape. Carefully, Khushi drew the cub out with his paw.

Every bone showed on the little body. The coat was dull and rough over prominent ribs, and the litterling staggered badly as he wobbled to Khushi and lay against the herder's forepaws.

Ratha stared down at the cub, feeling totally at a loss. Even if he had come from one of the clan's own females, she knew the drought was already straining the clan's resources.

Yet she couldn't help a twinge of pity for the cub's condition and awe for his tenacity. Having been taken from his mother at an early age and bumped around by a young herder who didn't know how to treat him, he should, by all rights, have been dead.

Fessran came alongside and peered at him. "Ratha, watch how he moves, tries to look at things. He reminds me of our own cubs."

Ratha felt that things were galloping ahead of her. "Firekeeper, he's too young and starved for us to make any judgment. And if there is one to be made, you are not the one to make it." She turned to Khushi once again. "Herder, you should have left him where he was. Take him back."

Fessran gave a derisive yowl. "You think his mother would accept him after Khushi's had him this long? We'd be lucky to even find her. And she may not want him back, especially now. The dry weather is also pressing the Un-Named."

Ratha eyed the Firekeeper. Fessran crouched down to

nuzzle and lick the orphan. She wouldn't have a family this year, and Ratha knew she wanted to raise cubs. That, plus the memory of Nyang's death and the loss of her treeling . . .

"If you get your scent on him too, we'll never get him back where he belongs," Ratha said.

"I think you're fooling yourself about that, clan leader," Fessran answered softly.

Ratha became aware that Khushi was watching the interchange between her and Fessran with unabashed curiosity. "Herder," she said, "go back to the three-horns. Fessran and I have some thinking to do. And if you are tempted to nurse any more Un-Named litterlings, tell me first."

When she looked back at Fessran, the Firekeeper lay on her side, the cub curled up against her belly. "I wish I could feed him," she said wistfully.

"I wish Khushi had never found him," Ratha growled. "Soft as dung indeed! Fessran, if you must play mother, ask Bira if you will be able to help with her litter. She came into heat early, and I can tell by her scent that the mating's taken."

"At least you're sure Bira's will have that cursed light in the eyes you're always looking for." Fessran looked up, her paw resting lightly on the orphan. "You bullied me into giving up Shongshar's cubs. Were you really that convinced that they were witless? If the Un-Named one that Khushi saw is the female I fostered, maybe she has more wits about her than you think. Perhaps we should trail her and find out."

Ratha said nothing, wondering if she should make Fessran remember the blank stare of Shongshar's daughter on the morning she had taken both young ones from Fessran's fostering.

"We can't get distracted by this," she said. "At least until the drought breaks. I'm not going to waste effort trailing an Un-Named female." Ratha paused. "And even if I was mistaken and her eyes show the gift we value, she is of Shongshar's blood and breed. Khushi said she had the long teeth. Would you want another like Shongshar to rise again in the clan?"

She saw the Firekeeper close her eyes and then lick the scars on her chest and upper foreleg. Fessran trembled for a minute, remembering. Then she withdrew herself from around the cub.

"What are you going to do with him?" she said gruffly.

"Khushi is to return him to the place he was found. If we leave him alone, his mother might reclaim him."

Mournfully Fessran said, "If I could just give him a good bellyful of milk . . .

Ratha sighed. "All right. I'll let Khushi feed him the way he did before." She sent Fessran to get Khushi. When the young herder arrived, she told him to bring the litterling to her once it was fed. She and Fessran went back to the herd and waited until Khushi returned with the orphan.

Ratha looked at the cub and wished that the young of the clan and of the Un-Named didn't look so much alike. *It is not only that their cubs resemble ours. They are so close to us, it makes me tremble. The only difference is behind the eyes. I have asked so many times why it is so, but no one can answer.*

Khushi put the youngster down, stretched his jaws, and complained. "He already feels heavy. And I'll be traveling with a dry tongue and a half-empty belly."

"Which is small punishment for sharing clan meat with one outside the clan and not telling me," said Ratha firmly. "Even if the meat came from your own belly and if the other is a cub."

Khushi sighed and agreed. He picked up the cub, started to trot away.

"Wait." The voice was Fessran's. Ratha narrowed her eyes at the Firekeeper.

"Let me go with him, clan leader," Fessran said. "You can spare me from tending the Red Tongue for a few days. I want to be sure we do the best we can for this cub. When Khushi's jaws start aching, he'll be tempted to leave the litterling anywhere."

Ratha was tempted to argue. In truth, she did need Fessran at her post, especially if there was an attack or an emergency. Other Firekeepers were good, but Fessran had the most experience with the Red Tongue.

"There's something else, clan leader," Fessran added. "I hate the thought of leaving my lost treeling behind. Maybe I can take one last look before we get too far from clan ground."

Ratha considered this. If Fessran did by chance find her treeling, that might cheer her up and take her mind off Un-Named cubs. But letting Fessran go with Khushi might not be the best idea. The Firekeeper clearly wanted to adopt the foundling, and letting her stay near the cub would only encourage her to disobey.

She knew Fessran had caught the look in her eyes, for the other's tail shivered, and she stared away. Ratha felt ashamed for doubting her friend. Her gaze rested on the fading scars that parted the Firekeeper's sandy coat.

Shongshar's slash had been intended for Ratha. Fessran had taken it.

Yet Ratha knew she would be faltering in her role as clan leader if she didn't admit her suspicions. What was it in the wretched litterling that touched Fessran so? She couldn't see anything promising about him, and the thought of his possible parentage made her shudder.

"Go look for your treeling, Fessran," she said. "Help Khushi if he needs it, but remember, this is his responsibility, not yours."

She knew from the slight twitch that narrowed one of Fessran's eyes that her words had done no good. She could feel the rift between them deepening. She wanted to reach across, somehow draw Fessran back, but it was not the right moment or place. The animals waited, dusty and stamping. The herders started to stare.

"Both of you go before the day gets too hot," Ratha said roughly, and turned back to the herd, not wanting to look as Khushi trotted away carrying the cub and Fessran followed.

CHAPTER 6

THAKUR'S RETURN JOURNEY to the coast went more quickly because he knew the trail. Again he emerged from the coastal forest onto meadows crowning high cliffs and traveled north along bluffs and ridges until late one evening, when he came to the beach and the jetty. In the scrub behind a bluff overlooking the ocean, he discovered a hollow between two boulders, made himself a nest, and slept.

In the morning, he awoke and took Aree up to a wooded area in the foothills behind the bluff, where the treeling could forage for leaves and insects. When she had eaten her fill, he started back to the beach, intending to seek out the young stranger who lived among the seamares.

The late morning sun warmed his back, making him feel loose limbed and lazy. Aree was snoozing in the hollow behind his shoulders; he could hear her gentle snoring and feel her wobble as he padded along. He grinned to himself, enjoying the feeling of her fingers gripping his fur and her small but comforting weight on his back.

Then the treeling tensed. He felt her fingers clench

just as a warning rattle of brush made him flatten his ears. In the next instant a rust-and-black form sprang at him from the side, landing half across his back. He heard teeth click as jaws snapped at Aree. The treeling scrambled onto his head, her hindquarters hanging over his muzzle, blinding him. But the strong tang of seamare mixed with female cat-scent told him who the attacker was.

With a shake of his head, he jolted Aree sideways so he could see again and at the same time flung himself onto his back, bringing his rear claws into play against his opponent's belly. He felt her scrabble on top of him, lunging for the treeling. With a screech, Aree bounded away and up the nearest sapling, where she clung, swaying as the slender tree bent.

Now Thakur could concentrate on subduing his attacker. She leaped over him, but just as she landed he rolled over and snagged her hindquarters with his foreclaws, knocking her to the ground. He grabbed her around the middle, hauling himself onto her. Angrily she twisted herself back on him, but she had only one front paw to strike out with. He caught the flailing foreleg in his jaws, biting only hard enough to hold it still.

Tangled up and twisted around as she was, she could only wriggle and heave beneath him. He loosed one front paw to fend off her attempt to bite him, catching her under the jaw and shoving her head to the side.

Her jerks grew frantic, and the swirling sea green in her eyes grew stormy. Abruptly her pupils, expanded in rage, contracted to needle size. She fought him with a new and terrifying strength, but her efforts were unfocused, as if she no longer struggled against a flesh-and-blood enemy but against something within herself.

Thakur could only hold on as tightly as possible, keeping her rear legs pressed to the ground and her foreleg trapped in his mouth. He feared that if she did get free, she would attack him in a savage frenzy. Whatever he had wakened within her, he would have to contain it until the paroxysm passed.

At last her heaving became sporadic, and her struggles weakened. He loosened his grip, feeling her sag onto her side. He let her forepaw go and watched it flop. Panting, he sat and looked down at her. Once again she lay at his feet, defeated by the strange fit he had caused. This time, however, he didn't feel as guilty, although he was surprised. He had never thought she would dare attack him, even with the temptation of the treeling on his back. Perhaps Aree's smell proved too strong a lure. But the stranger was the one who had been caught.

Her lip twitched back, showing her upper fang. Her jaw trembled and her tongue moved. And then Thakur heard her voice.

"Stay away . . . from them. . . ."

As she spoke the first few syllables, he leaned closer, wondering if he was imagining words in her inarticulate moans. Her voice was harsh and breathy.

"I won't hurt you," Thakur answered, puzzled as to whom she meant. "I held you off from my treeling, but I mean you no harm."

She hadn't heard him. She stared ahead, her gaze milky, shrouded, hissing words in strange disconnected clumps.

". . . wish they had been born dead . . . do you want

her . . . she's witless . . . why did you do this to me
. . . why . . ."

The sounds were indeed words in the speech of the
Named, and he heard in them a pain and an eloquence
that made him shiver. Yet the voice that said them was
hollow and remote, as if she spoke without knowing what
she said.

Her lips fell back over her fangs and she was silent,
but her words still echoed in Thakur's mind. He paced
back and forth beside her in confusion. Who were those
she warned him to stay away from? Cubs? He looked at
her belly. No, she wasn't nursing a litter. And what had
she said about wishing "they" had been born dead? It
made no sense to him.

But the agony had come through all too clearly. She
whimpered deep in her throat, like a cub needing comfort. He lay down beside her, letting her feel his body
warmth. Instinctively, she squirmed toward him.
Though he wanted to move away because she was ungroomed and smelly, compassion overcame his disgust.
He nuzzled her behind the ears. It soothed her, and she
sank from confusion into sleep.

He wasn't sure how long the stranger lay curled up
with her back against him. Aree had gotten over her
fright and was starting to descend from the sapling when
the lame female stirred, this time into full wakefulness.
Again he nuzzled her behind the ears, purring to calm
her. She gave a startled jerk but did not scramble away.

She lifted her head to look at him.

"You're all right," Thakur said softly. "I promise I
won't let anyone hurt you. Do you have a name?"

The swirling green in her eyes seemed to surround and

engulf him with intensity. The fur on her brow rumpled, and he could see that his words only baffled her.

He repeated his soothing litany, seeing that the sound of his voice did calm her, but the words themselves meant nothing.

"You don't understand me," he said, dismayed. "You must. I heard you speak." But the veil of muteness had dropped upon her once again, and only cloudiness moved in those eyes. "It doesn't matter," he said softly, feeling her start to tremble. "Just rest here with me."

After a little while, she got up and shook herself, but she did not scamper away. She sat watching him while he indulged in a good stretch. A chirr overhead reminded him he still had a treeling to look after. Aree hung by her tail from a branch of the willowy sapling, looking doubtfully at Thakur's new acquaintance.

"She's not going to eat you," Thakur said, cajoling the treeling, but as Aree started to climb down, the lame female took several eager steps toward the sapling. Gently, but firmly, Thakur blocked her with his body. "Oh no, my hungry friend. Aree's not going to be your dinner."

When the stranger was stubborn and persisted, Thakur put a paw against her breast and pushed her away. "No," he hissed sharply, emphasizing it with a flash of teeth. She backed away, letting Aree climb nervously onto Thakur's nape, lying so flat that it felt as though she were trying to bury herself in his fur.

Again the stranger sidled toward him, but another emphatic negative halted her.

He knew she didn't understand him, but the sound of

his voice seemed to calm her, so he rambled on. "Look, I came here to learn about you, but since you can't or won't talk, why don't you just prowl around while I watch?"

She cocked her head at him, then limped a few steps away. He saw how she kept the crippled foreleg tucked underneath her chest.

"You should try to use that foot," he said, speaking his thought aloud. He came alongside her and pawed at her foreleg, trying to get her to extend the shrunken limb. Gently he took her foot in his mouth and pulled, testing how far he could stretch the contracted muscles.

She gave a sharp yowl of pain, wrenched her paw away from him.

"I didn't mean to hurt you. I'll be careful." He coaxed her into offering her foot again, although she gave a warning growl. Again he took it, pulled gently.

She tugged back with surprising strength in the wasted limb.

Stubbornly but gently, Thakur held on, purring to reassure her. "Easy," he said, talking around a mouthful of furred toes. "I just wanted to see how this has healed."

He turned the limb from side to side, also studying the collar of roughened fur that overlay scars from the injury that had crippled her. The scarring ran right down her neck to her breast. It looked like a bad bite, perhaps done to her when she was small. If fangs had penetrated a young cub's chest near the foreleg, they might have caused such a paralyzing injury.

But in her case, the part that gave the limb life and motion had somehow begun to heal. He could tell that by the way the leg jerked back against his jaws. The real problem was that her muscles had thinned and contracted while the leg was immobile.

The healer in Thakur wanted to tell the stranger that she might not have to spend the rest of her life hobbling about on three legs. The practical part of him knew he couldn't get this across to her without the use of words. Maybe if he could just show her—get her to stretch the leg and try using it.

But she had already grown impatient. She tugged her paw from his jaws and stalked away.

Thakur waited before he went after her, fearing she might hiss or try to drive him away, but she didn't. Considering the start of this encounter, it hadn't turned out all that badly, he concluded as he followed her. Perhaps she might accept him enough to show him the seabeasts she guarded.

Winding his way down through the thorny, scrubby brush of the slopes behind the bluff, Thakur kept to the lame female's track. He could hear her moving ahead of him, stopping and starting nervously. When she halted, he stayed back, not wanting to alarm her by moving too close. He paced himself by the uneven rhythm of her three-legged gait, slowing his own.

When they emerged onto the beach, she seemed less certain about wanting him to follow. He hung back, showing that he was willing to respect her privacy. After several stops, tail flicks, and doubtful stares in his direction, she let him trail her to a terrace near the seamares' jetty. She grimaced at him to stay there.

Obediently, he dropped down on his belly as she disappeared behind an outcrop of sandstone. He feared Aree might grow restive, but the treeling made herself a nest in the hollow between his nape and shoulder blades and was soon snoring lightly. Thoughts of the stranger chased themselves about in his mind. He remembered how her jaws had moved and her tongue formed speech while she lay in the grip of the fit that had seized her. Yet when she recovered, she was as mute as ever.

Thakur thought too of Ratha's swift pace and the trails she would be traveling. She and Fessran would soon arrive on the coast, and then others would come, creating a further disruption to the fragile balance of the life his strange friend had made for herself.

While he was still puzzling over it, he heard her footsteps approaching. He stayed down until she approached, then rose slowly. Again that sea-green stare held him until she swung around and went ahead, letting him follow. He could catch the odor of seamare in the wind, teasing his whiskers, and wondered if the stranger would allow him near the wave-wallowers. To gain the trust he wanted, he had to show her that he would do nothing threatening.

As he trotted down onto the beach, he saw her rolling on her back in dung that smelled overwhelmingly of seamare. She wriggled around in the mess until she had worked it well into her coat, gave herself a shake, and stood up. He noticed that she had thoughtfully left a pile for him. Obviously this was a requirement for approaching her charges.

He could see at once that this made sense. The odoriferous stuff would obliterate any trace of his smell, making him seem harmless to the seamares. Some of Thakur's own herders made a practice of rolling in the manure of animals they kept, claiming that made the creatures less difficult to manage. Thakur himself had never cared for the idea.

He didn't much like the idea of it now either. The lame female gave an impatient flip of her tail. When he tried to walk around the dung, she showed her teeth. It was either roll or give up. Thakur decided to roll. But Aree certainly wouldn't tolerate being smeared with the stuff. Treelings liked to keep themselves clean.

"If you don't mind, I'd better find a safe place for my treeling first," he said, hoping she might understand his intent if not his words. He nosed Aree, then flicked a whisker in the direction they had just come. Quickly he left the beach and backtracked up the trail until he found a gnarled cypress high enough to keep the treeling safe from any ground-prowling meat eaters. Aree clambered up, grumbling a little, and hid in a hollow several tail lengths overhead.

Thakur found the lame female waiting where he had left her. Though she cast a hungry look down the trail, he was relieved to see that she did not go after his hidden treeling. The seamare dung was as pungent as ever, lying in a heap at his feet. He hoped she might have forgotten, but she hadn't. He rolled.

He had assumed that the seamares ate sea grass or other plant fodder, like the herdbeasts he knew. The smell of the manure told him that the creatures had a much more varied diet, possibly including flesh or fish. Herdbeast dung was not repellent to him, but that of meat eaters other than his own kind carried a disgusting tang. He had to force himself to cover his coat with the seamare smell, wondering how he was ever going to clean up before he recovered Aree. And if he met any of the Named while wearing such a wretched odor . . . well, he decided not to think about that.

The female took one sniff and then led him to a group of seamares. He kept as close to her as he dared and tried to put his feet down silently. The seamares lay looking like logs washed ashore, but as he approached, ears twitched and heads lifted. The small eyes seemed to grow colder, and the tusks Thakur had glimpsed from a distance seemed larger. He told himself that one who challenged three-horns should have no fear of these clumsy wave-wallowers. But he was grateful for the odor that hung about him and disguised his smell.

The change in odor seemed to put the lame female more at ease, and he remembered how his scent-mark had triggered her first fit.

Thakur followed his companion as she limped close to one seamare, who lay at the edge of the herd with a half-grown youngster. With his odd friend standing nearby, he could walk close to the pair and examine them.

Ratha's description of these animals as "duck-footed dapplebacks" wasn't that far off, he decided. Their stout, black toes had scaled skin and a fold of webbing between them. Their bodies looked much the same as those of dapplebacks', although broader and chunkier. The seamares' coats were dense and velvety.

Thakur was startled to see the mother seamare take a large clam from a heap she had gathered, crack the shell, and deliberately lay it aside. With a glance at Thakur, the lame female set about prying the meat out of the mollusk with her good forepaw and her teeth. He thought she would eat it all, but halfway through she lifted her head and stared at him, then brought him a fragment of shell with meat still attached.

He did his best to rasp off the rubbery clam flesh and gulp it down, though it made a wad in his throat that threatened to choke him. He felt he could tolerate it, though he was grateful she didn't offer him any more. She watched him while he ate, and he in turn tried to read those odd opaque eyes.

As he trailed her among the seamares for the rest of the day, he became more and more convinced that the dullness she showed was only on the surface. Beneath lay a sharp and perceptive intelligence, though one that worked in a very different way than his own.

The question of her apparent muteness rose again in his mind. It wasn't that she could not make sounds, for he heard her use a wide variety of vocalizations. And her tongue could form words; he had heard her speak as clearly as one of the Named.

And when he spoke, as he did once in a while to himself, her reaction was more than just irritation or annoyance. Even as she turned her back on his words, he caught a look of longing in her eyes and a movement of her jaws that halted abruptly, as if she had caught herself trying to imitate him. Thakur noticed this but did nothing about it. He was unsure what he could do and was too taken up with studying the seamares to devote much thought to it.

After he had been on the beach for several days and had satisfied much of his curiosity about the wave-wallowers themselves, he turned his attention to the one who guarded them.

He spoke, as if muttering to himself, but this time he watched his strange friend, not letting her see his scrutiny. A fleeting look of something akin to despair passed through her eyes.

"You want to speak," said Thakur, talking to her directly. "Why don't you try?"

He said his name, trying to get her to repeat it, but she only ducked her head and would not meet his gaze.

"When you fell on your side that day I came, you spoke. Don't you remember? Or were you just making sounds that had no meaning for you?"

She crouched, looking away, but he could tell by the way her ears swiveled that she was listening. Her tail tip trembled and began to wag in confusion.

"You are Named. I know you are." The fierce conviction in his voice frightened Newt. Her ears twitched back, and the green in her eyes became turbulent, cutting off any sight he might have glimpsed of their depths. He softened his tone, knowing it was useless to force her.

She stared up at him from her crouch, and a pleading look came into her eyes. Again her mouth opened, her tongue writhed, but no sound emerged. Her eyes grew shuttered as she closed her mouth, but there was a spark of pain in them sharp enough to penetrate the dullness of her gaze. Thakur wondered if his efforts were adding to her inner torment.

He could only fall silent once again, wondering if he would ever reach her.

CHAPTER 7

To lessen the disturbance that arose in his new friend whenever he spoke in the tongue of his people, Thakur tried to use only the instinctive cat-noises and body language of his kind. In gesture he had to be careful too, for the Named had overlaid their natural movements and signals with ones that had added meaning. If he strayed over the boundary, he confused his new companion. Clan language in all its forms had obviously been denied to her, yet he could see she hungered for some means of expression. She was not so much mute as she was trapped, caught between a desperate desire to have language and something that frightened her away from it.

His intuition urged him to speak to her and coax her to respond, as if she were one whose speech had been halted by sickness or the forgetfulness of age. When he saw the panic that started up in her eyes whenever he spoke, he knew it wouldn't work; she was too frightened.

And so for her sake, he too became mute, suppressing his impulses to talk whenever he was with her. It was a strange and difficult thing for him to do. The unsaid words seemed to lie in his breast with a leaden weight, pulling him down. After a day or so of self-enforced silence, his mind rebelled, harassing him with arguments against his choice. When his jaw remained shut, it punished him with a strange weariness that left him feeling dull and draggy. The sound of the wind was muffled and distant, as if his ears were stuffed with fur. He fought to keep himself from falling into a trancelike state.

His only respite was when he retreated from the beach to find Aree in whatever tree he had perched her and take her on his back to forage. Her chirrs and chattering removed the barrier his will had set up, and he talked to her in a gush of words like a dammed stream suddenly freed to flow again. But once she had been installed for the day in her refuge, Thakur resumed his silence.

Just when he felt he would *have* to say something aloud, the muffled, distanced feeling retreated and he found himself hearing, seeing, and smelling the world about him with a new sharpness and clarity. The pressure to speak his thoughts was no longer so overwhelming. He felt more "outside" himself than he had ever done, more a part of the world and aware of it.

He began to sense that the gift of language was not entirely a gift, that it took something in return as payment. Words and thoughts controlled the way he saw things, coloring his actions and feelings at the price of raw clarity and the intensity of the moment. Was this the way those whom the clan called the Un-Named saw and felt? And the lame female? Did those eyes that looked so dull at times actually look out upon the world with a perception perhaps narrowed, but much keener than his own?

And then something odd happened that upset all his preconceptions. He was lying on his side on one of the upper terraces above the crowded mass of seamares. The lame female lay with him, stretched out in the warm sun. Thakur felt tired but tranquil. He had gained her trust and her friendship.

Gently his companion reached out with her good fore-paw and patted his jowls. He thought for a moment that she was just playing, but she touched him again in the same place with a stroking motion of her paw. Her lower jaw trembled, opened.

The realization broke on him like a cold wave, leaving him trembling with chill and excitement. She didn't want him to be silent. She wanted him to talk! And she was asking him to pull her from her own silence, even though it might force her to face something she greatly feared.

It took him a little while to find his voice again, and it felt creaky from disuse. "Thank you," he said softly in the words of gratitude used among the Named.

Her ears flicked back, but she wiggled herself a little closer to him on her side, her eyes expectant.

"Where do I start?" he asked her. Again she patted his jowls. "Anything?"

Anything. He talked to her, watching her ears. They would prick forward, then flatten abruptly, but then start to swivel forward once again. He told her stories about his life with the clan, his work teaching cubs, his adventures, how he had found his treeling. It didn't matter that the words had no meaning to her; she just wanted to hear them. Thakur was reminded that clan cubs heard their parents speaking from the moment they were born.

And so from muteness he went to a flood of talk. There was an almost terrified eagerness in the young female's face as she began trying to imitate him. But nothing came out. Thakur encouraged her attempts, but it did not increase their success. Nothing worked—simple words, phrases, his name: They elicited only a frenzied struggle and then a strange, sad subsidence.

Had those words that had come from her tongue during her fit been a product of his own imagination? Again he heard the hollow, breathy voice in his mind. *Stay away from them*, she had said. *Why did you do this to me? Why? I wish they had been born dead. . . . She's witless.*

Strange, disjointed phrases—yet they might hide a chilling history. And she had spoken them once. Perhaps she could speak the same words again. An uneasy feeling made him hesitate, but he could see no other way. He chose the most innocuous of her utterances. Settling close beside her, he caught her gaze and then slowly said, "Stay away from them. Stay away." He repeated the phrase, making it rhythmic. She followed the pattern, bobbing her head slightly to the beat of his speech, as clan cubs did when trying to learn something difficult.

And then the first word came from her mouth. "Stay," she blurted, and then, softer but clearer, "Stay."

Thakur was lavish in his praise, trying to overcome the uncertainty that showed in her eyes at the sound of her own voice. "Stay," he said, then got up and moved away. When she moved to follow, he pushed her back, making her sit where she was, hoping she would get the idea of what the word meant. It was an odd combination of teaching a clan cub, who could understand that words had meaning, and training a treeling, who understood them only as commands. After many repetitions, he could get her to remain in place with the one word and, after more work, could keep her from approaching him with the phrase "Stay away."

The afternoon shadows grew longer across the rocks as Thakur drilled his new student. Abruptly, after he had given her the command one last time and she had obeyed it, she sat down with her brow furrowed.

"What's the matter?" he asked, forgetting himself.

She looked at him blankly. "Away. Stay away. Stay away from them." Panic rose like a storm in her eyes, and the words came quickly, hammered out as fast as she could say them. "Stay away from them, why did you do this to me, do you really want them, she's witless . . . she's witless . . . I wish they had been born dead . . . born dead . . . born dead . . ."

Pupils enlarging, she backed away from Thakur, who was already regretting his choice of teaching methods. Somehow he had set her off again; she had gone into the terrifying world that only she could see.

He expected her to stiffen and topple as she had done in the first two incidents, but this time she lunged, screaming and swiping at an invisible enemy. Then she turned tail and fled, diving among the rocks, scrabbling as fast as she could go.

Thakur pursued her, grateful that she had chosen a path uphill instead of down into the midst of the sea-mares. But terror gave her speed, despite her three-legged run, and he caught up with her only when lack of breath slowed her headlong dash. Trying to be as gentle as he could, he knocked her sideways with his shoulder, then followed as she tumbled into a clump of weeds.

She lay on her side, her legs stiff, shuddering and

trembling. He lay down with her, licking her behind the ears until she grew still. At last she lifted her head and stared at him, looking bewildered and lost. Her mouth opened.

"No," he said softly. "Don't try any more. It hurts you too much."

A stubborn glint appeared behind the swirling fear and forced its way through into the colors of her eyes. She jerked her mouth open and almost in defiance said, "Stay!" She flinched as if someone might strike her and for an instant went rigid, making Thakur afraid she had fallen back into her illness. She drove her claws into the ground and bared her teeth.

Abruptly her eyes cleared. She turned to Thakur, who was starting to rise. "Stay," she begged, convincing him now that she understood the meaning of the word.

"All right." He sighed, flopped down, and offered her a shoulder on which to rest her drooping head. He felt her go limp, as if exhausted. He felt weary and emotionally battered himself. Was it worth trying to teach her speech if everything was going to be such a struggle?

As if in reply, her good forepaw came up and patted his jowls, as if to say *I will fight what scares me. I want to learn.*

The barrier within her against learning to speak had weakened. Thakur used only the words in those few phrases she had spoken. Once she understood those, he was uncertain what to try next. Among the first things that clan cubs learned were their names. She didn't have a name, as far as he knew. Or did she? Having proved herself much more self-aware than he had assumed, she might well have some image of herself or some sound that served the same purpose. But how to get it out of her?

He began the obvious way: by teaching her his own name. But here he ran into trouble. It was difficult to get across to her the idea that the sound *Thakur* meant himself. She didn't understand any of the paw or tail gestures the Named would use to emphasize the idea of someone speaking about himself. And then the notion hit him. There were certain times when the Named felt most individual and personal. One of these was during mating, but Thakur decided that such an approach would have problems that he didn't want to deal with. The other time was when someone was grooming, cleaning and smoothing their fur.

Despite the tang of seamare in his coat, he set about licking himself, trying not to be too thorough, for fear of having to roll in the creatures' dung once again. She wandered up, sat down, and watched. Every few strokes, he paused and said his name. Her head cocked to one side. He smelled the fur along his back, taking a deep, noisy breath, and then said his name again. She sniffed him, then began to wash herself, but he quickly put a paw out to stop her. He didn't want her to get the idea that *Thakur* meant the action of grooming oneself.

It took a little time, but gradually she understood what he was trying to get across.

"Thakur," she said shyly, then sniffed his coat and touched him with a paw. Again he praised her, then sniffed her coat and stroked her with his pad.

"What is your name?" he asked.

She opened her mouth, closed it again, looked down in confusion. The fur between her eyes furrowed. He could see she knew what he wanted but was at a loss to express it.

"Stay," she said, and then bounded away. He checked his impulse to go after her. This departure was different from the last. She wasn't fleeing in terror; she had some purpose, though what, he had no idea. After she had been gone for what seemed a long while, he decided to go after her.

But no sooner had he gotten to his feet than she reappeared, carrying something limp in her mouth. When she put the thing down, it wriggled, throwing its body into sinuous curves. Thakur blinked and stared. She'd brought him a live newt.

He sat down, baffled, wondering what this action had to do with the lesson he'd been trying to teach. Was this supposed to be a reward because he'd done something that pleased her? He leaned over, sniffing the moist creature and grimacing with disgust. He wondered if he would offend her if he didn't eat it. Perhaps he should at least try.

Her good forepaw batted him away. He sat up, cocking his head to one side. If the newt wasn't meant as food, why did she bring it?

She pawed herself, then poked the creature with her toe, making it thrash. It writhed on the dry rock, covering itself with sand, but not before Thakur saw that the rust-black and orange markings on its moist skin approximated the color of his friend's fur. He thought about her eagerness for words, for names. And that was what he had asked her.

By showing him the newt, she was telling him her name in the only way she knew.

"Newt?" he said, touching her with his forefoot. She pawed her evident namesake once again and danced around so excitedly that he had to intercede to keep her from accidentally squashing the it. Newt. She certainly hadn't flattered herself by the choice.

She imitated the sound of her name, attached it to the creature. Again Thakur praised her, which resulted in more repetitions, more dancing, and the near trampling of the poor newt.

"All right. Why don't you take that animal back where you found it, since I'm not hungry right now." Thakur jerked his muzzle in the direction from which she had brought it.

She looked at him wide eyed. "Thakur stay," she said, then scooped the sand-covered newt up in her jaws and dashed off on three legs.

Grinning, he sat where he was until she returned. He hoped the creature had survived the teaching session. He didn't like to see things killed unless he was ready to eat them.

It was midmorning on the next day, and the two sat together near her cave. Thakur cocked his head at Newt and switched his tail in bafflement. He had risen feeling self-satisfied by what he had taught her the previous day, but now he was reconsidering.

"Thakur, stay," Newt said. When he did as she asked, a mournful look came into her eyes, and she stamped a rear foot on the ground. Clearly, she wanted him to follow, but she was stuck with only one phrase.

"No, it's *Thakur come,*" he corrected.

"Thakur stay," Newt said again, with a stamp and an impatient grimace.

"I'm not coming until you figure out what the difference is and use the right word."

"Yarrr," was Newt's response.

"Yarrr, yourself. The word is *come.* I've told you that more times than I have hairs."

She turned her back on him and stalked off, but she didn't stay away for long. He could see by the little flickers in her eyes that she had something she wanted to show him.

She came back and tried, "Come stay."

Thakur grinned. "Can't do both."

"Thakur . . . Thakur . . ." Newt faltered, lost. Her ears twitched back. With a quick pounce, she seized his tail, pulled it, then made a three-legged pirouette in front of him, swatted him across the muzzle with her tail, and took off.

Thakur was several steps after her before he realized he'd been tricked. "You won't learn to talk if you keep distracting me!" he yowled after her, but she was beyond earshot. He sighed and kept trotting.

Coming over a dune, he spotted her on the shore of the shallow lagoon that lay south of the beach. The early morning fog had lifted, letting sunlight spill onto the sand and across the wavelets.

As he came down the sandy slope, Newt bounded over to him. "Thakur, come," she said triumphantly, then limped vigorously into the water. Welcoming a chance to cool himself, he followed, wading into the shallows until the wavelets lapped his belly. His casual glance at

Newt sharpened as he realized that she was not just playing cub-games in the lagoon, as he had first thought.

He watched with growing interest as she spread herself out in the water. Using her hind feet and tail in a sculling motion that reminded him of how river otters swam, she glided forward, the waves forming a V-shaped wake in front of her ears. Her waterborne grace and agility surprised him. And then he saw that she no longer held her crippled foreleg tightly against her chest. The push and swell of the water drew the limb gently outward, and she moved it slightly to counteract each stroke of her good forepaw.

Thakur felt his eyes opening wider. He knew that water could be healing, for he had learned that the best treatment for bruises and sprains was to lie and let the limb dangle in the cold, running flow of a stream. The pain and swelling would fade much faster. If it could heal small hurts, he thought, perhaps it might give strength back to a withered forelimb.

Newt made a few lazy turns, then surfaced near him, her whiskers dripping. "Thakur come," she chirped, then swam away. He followed, suddenly self-conscious about his clumsy paddling as compared to her elegant glide. Again she slid by in front of his nose like a fish. Her tail tip lifted, flipped a sprinkle of water into his face, and he spluttered, putting his feet down on the bottom.

"I swim about as well as you talk," he said, as her head lifted again. "How do you do that?" He tried to float with his head down but immediately got a noseful of brackish seawater. He grimaced, coughing and drawing back his whiskers. Newt floated near him, swishing her tail lazily, her head up. She blew at him through her mouth and nose with a breathy, hissing sound. Still blowing, she ducked under again. A welter of bubbles boiled around her muzzle and ears.

Thakur watched. When she surfaced, he blew back at her. She grinned, slapped her good forepaw on top of his head, dunked him under, and held him. For one confused moment, he struggled, wondering why she was trying to drown him. Then he knew that she had decided to teach him in her own fashion. With a strong breath, he blew out the water flooding his mouth and nose. She let him up.

He dunked Newt in turn, watching her breath surface as bubbles. Moving away from her, he tried putting his face in the water. The first few times he ended up with brine in his throat, but he began to master the trick of controlling his breathing to overcome the feeling of suffocation and keep water out of his mouth and nose.

Thakur opened his eyes in the clear water of the lagoon. He could see somewhat blurrily, but he could make out objects. There was Newt, hanging in the water nearby, her fur forming a soft halo about her as currents teased it away from her body. He felt the water push against his face, tug unpleasantly at his sensitive nose and brow whiskers, and seep over his jowls into his mouth. Lifting his head, he shook the water out of his ears. This was interesting, but it would take some getting used to.

Newt drifted into the shallows near him. She looked up at him, then pawed the water with her forefeet in imitation of his paddling. Both forefeet. He stared at her two paws, the good one splashing vigorously, the other feeble but moving. It hadn't been just his imagination or wishful thinking. Her leg wasn't as useless as it appeared.

"Newt," he said softly, nudging her. "Look." She stared down, following the odd jerks of her crippled forelimb through the water. With a self-conscious grimace, she tugged the leg to her chest and held it there.

"No. What you were doing before; that was good." Gently, Thakur pawed her foot away from her chest, coaxing her to let the forelimb drift free. He batted her limb back and forth in a small arc beneath the water, then took her foot in his mouth, trying to see how far the tightened muscles would stretch. This time she did not jerk away.

With his nose underwater, Thakur moved the shrunken limb back and forth until Newt caught on to the idea. "Good," he said, sneezing brine out of his whiskers. "You do it now."

She managed several short, jerky sweeps. He saw it was harder for her to move the leg intentionally than it had been when she was just swimming. She persisted, even when the leg began trembling. He made her stop, then encouraged her to swim again by making a few clumsy paddle-strokes. She glided around him, then looked up. Again she pawed the water. "Newt . . . ?"

Thakur grinned. She was so good at this water play that of course she would want to know the word for it. "Swim," Thakur told her.

"Newt swim," she said. "Thakur swim." She glided around him, twisting and turning.

"Good." He purred and gave her a soggy nuzzle.

"Good," Newt echoed.

He licked her behind the ears, then ducked to avoid another splash.

Later he had her do more exercise with the leg, sweeping it back and forth as far as it would go against the resistance of the water. He felt he had found something important, although he was not exactly sure how it might work.

CHAPTER 8

FESSRAN AND KHUSHI were gone from clan ground for many days. For Ratha, those days dragged like the weary herders' feet, as the weather grew hotter and the trails dustier.

She lay in late-afternoon shade that felt as hot as open sun. She panted, feeling worn out and worried. She wished she had delayed Thakur from returning to the lake-of-waves and its odd inhabitant. The task of controlling herdbeasts made restive by thirst and flies was a wearying one, in addition to her other duties as leader. And the new water source she thought would last had begun to fail.

Both Thakur and Fessran were gone. She let her jaw sag as she panted. Letting them both go had been a bad decision. But how was she to know that Khushi would turn up with a stolen cub from the ranks of the Un-

Named, who might well have sprung from the loins of her bitterest enemy? Could anyone blame her if she wanted that litterling off clan ground as fast as possible and shred the consequences!

Letting Fessran go with Khushi was only a quicker way to speed him off with his unwanted burden. Ratha sighed. Not a good decision. Even if all Fessran wanted was her lost treeling—but Ratha couldn't bring herself to believe that.

She lay with her tail flicking, thinking about the good and bad parts of what Thakur had told her before he left. The good part was the spring. Thakur had described how underground water flowed from a series of cracks in a cliff that lay just behind the beach where he had found the duck-footed dapplebacks. With its source deep in the earth, the spring would run even when everything else went dry. The spring watered thickets where three-horns could browse and patches of meadow that would do for the dapplebacks.

The bad part was that the Named would have to leave clan ground for as long as the drought lasted. Ratha laid her chin down on grass that once would have cooled but now crackled. The journey there would be exhausting. She thought of the river drives and the prospect of increasing the tumult, dust, and weariness over days of traveling.

Before she uprooted the clan, she must see the spring for herself, to be absolutely sure it would support the needs of the Named and their herds through the drought. She wanted to study the wave-wallowers themselves, along with the Un-Named one who lived among them.

Soon she would follow Thakur's tracks to this great, brine-filled lake. She itched to be gone. But she meant to take Fessran with her, and the Firekeeper had not yet returned. She sighed and laid her nose on her paws instead of the scratchy grass.

Though the clan would be losing its leader and chief Firekeeper for a short time, Ratha felt that this journey was essential, and she needed Fessran's opinion as much as her own. She had already spoken to the older herder, Cherfan, about taking over clan leadership while she was gone. And Bira, Fessran's second-in-command among the Firekeepers, had overcome much of her shyness and had grown skilled in the management of the Red Tongue and those who kept it.

Fessran's absence would give Bira a chance to emerge from the chief Firekeeper's shadow and show her abilities. Cherfan was a strong, experienced herder and respected by all. Ratha did not think her own and Fessran's absence would be long enough to cause difficulty; at the slow rate the river was dropping, things would remain stable enough until she had found a place for the clan.

Fessran and Khushi surprised her by arriving later that same afternoon. A herder ran ahead, bringing the news to her and waking her from her sleep in the shade. As soon as the two travelers came into sight, Ratha saw Fessran was still missing her treeling. Khushi's jaws, thankfully, were empty. With a rising purr, she invited them to stretch out beside her.

When both had rested and groomed, Ratha asked how they had fared on the journey. She noticed that Fessran let Khushi do most of the talking.

"We didn't find the cub's mother. I didn't expect that we would," Khushi said matter-of-factly. "We left him in a safe place. If she's still in the area, she'll find him."

Ratha glanced at Fessran in surprise. "You agreed to let Khushi do that?"

Fessran seemed preoccupied. She was slow to respond, and her voice sounded distant.

"We couldn't think of anything else," she said. "The mother was gone, and we couldn't find her. We would only have frightened her more if we had. And you would have chewed our ears to scraps if you saw us bringing the cub back." Fessran stretched out in the shade and began grooming her belly. "Anyway, I did some thinking while I was on the trail and decided you were right. There was no use in making a fuss about this Un-Named cub when we will have our own."

But you won't be having cubs this season, Ratha thought.

She tongued her own fur, wondering where her feeling of uneasiness had suddenly come from. Nothing in Fessran's smell or manner alarmed her, yet she had the sense that something wasn't right. Well, it wasn't like Fessran to give up fighting for something she cared about. Not so abruptly.

What are you complaining about? she asked herself crossly. *I made Fessran obey me, which is something I've had trouble doing ever since I became leader.*

Yet this time Fessran's willfulness had seemed to echo her own conscience. She might just be wrong about this litterling. Her judgment might have been too hasty and too harsh. And not just with him . . .

She felt slightly dismayed, as if her conscience had

given in too easily, just as Fessran had. As if the stronger and not so likable part of her had won out.

I don't like it, but that's what made me clan leader.

She decided to forget about the cub. There were other things to think about; new journeys to plan. Fessran would come with her, and perhaps the time together would allow her to mend the rift in their friendship. Warming to the idea, she laid out the prospect of the coastward journey to the Firekeeper.

Fessran, however, was curiously unenthusiastic, and when Ratha said she wanted to leave the following day, the look in Fessran's eyes was one of reluctance.

"Are you sure you want to leave so soon?" Fessran asked.

"I have to see Thakur's spring for myself, and that must be done quickly."

"That makes sense," Fessran agreed, though her voice sounded flat. "Why do you want me, though? I'm not a herder. You and Thakur are more skilled at judging if a place is fit for keeping three-horns."

"You were a herder before I gave you Firekeeper leadership. Fessran, I can't make this judgment alone. You and Thakur are the ones I trust the most. If I must tear the Named from clan ground, let me have some hope that I am doing what is right."

"You haven't had doubts about other things, clan leader," Fessran replied, and the way she said it told Ratha she had not forgotten the Un-Named cub. Before Ratha's ears could flatten, Fessran yawned widely. "All right, I'll come. But give me at least a day to rest. My shoulder aches and my pads feel like I've walked across every rock in the world. I just want to be left alone to sleep."

Fessran got what she wanted, and Khushi soon joined her in the dense shade beneath a pine that stood apart from the other trees in and around the meadow. It was Bonechewer's grave-tree. Ratha wondered if Fessran had chosen the spot deliberately, so that the clan leader would not come near.

She was surprised by the strength of anger and sadness that weighted her steps as she padded away. She remembered her dead mate too well: the gleaming copper coat, the amber eyes, and the voice that was sardonic yet caring. And she remembered the faces of their cubs and especially the face of their daughter, Thistle-chaser. The blank, bewildered stare of her own litterling suddenly became the equally empty gaze of the Un-Named orphan she had ordered Khushi to abandon.

Toward sunset something drew her to the pine again. If Fessran was as weary as she had sounded, she would still be asleep, and Ratha planned not to wake her. But when she arrived near the grave-tree, she heard only one set of rumbling snores, and they were Khushi's. Fessran had gone.

Ratha sniffed the ground around the pine. Her first instinct was to track the Firekeeper, but suddenly she grew disgusted with herself. Being clan leader was turning her suspicious and sour, ruining an old and valued friendship. Did she really have a good reason not to trust Fessran? Did she have to know where everyone was and what he was doing at every moment?

She shook herself, grimaced, and trotted away.

Fessran returned, in good time to supervise the lighting of watchfires for the night. Ratha watched the slim, sandy form trotting from one Firekeeper to the next, giving advice, instructions, and seeing that the fires were kept properly fed yet contained. Ratha let her suspicions drop with a sigh of relief. Wherever Fessran went was her own business. She worked hard and well for the clan. There might be mutterings about what she had done in the past, but she had done more than enough to redeem herself, and no one could fault her now.

In the morning, Ratha woke Fessran and met with Cherfan and Bira. If this journey yielded the refuge the Named sought, she said to the older herder, then Fessran would return with instructions to guide the clan, and Cherfan was to bring them under her direction. After the Firekeeper leader gave some brief advice to Bira, Fessran and Ratha set out on their journey to the coast.

Days later, Thakur approached the lone tree at the clearing that lay inland from the beach. He smelled places where two of the Named had chin-rubbed against rough bark. Ratha's scent he knew well, and Fessran's had an acrid, smoky undertone that told of her place as Firekeeper leader. They had both passed this way not long ago.

He also sniffed an odor that surprised him and re-awakened his belly-rumbles: fresh meat. Either the two females had just eaten or they were carrying prey. His ears cocked forward. He knew Ratha had learned to hunt during her exile from the clan, but the smell told him that this was no wild prey. The meat came from a herd-beast. How could they have dragged it all that way and kept it from turning rank? Perhaps one of them was just carrying a small piece for him in her mouth. His own watered at the thought.

Thakur circled back to follow their trail, then hesitated. Ratha and Fessran's arrival meant company and perhaps food, but it also meant that the time the clan leader had allotted him to study Newt and her sea-creatures was gone. He felt now that he might have enough knowledge to try herding the seamares. Ratha would be eager to test his suggestion. But this would mean more intrusion into Newt's life. Thakur sensed that the place she had made for herself was precarious and could easily be destroyed.

The smell of the two Named females and the tantalizing odor of food teased him onward, and he trotted after them with Aree riding on his nape. Soon after he broke out of thinning forest into coastal meadow, he caught sight of two tawny backs moving ahead of him through the grass. He didn't need to call, for the wind had carried his smell ahead of him. He saw both figures turn, their ears and whiskers lifting at the sight of him. But although he smelled food, neither Ratha nor Fessran carried anything in their mouths. His belly gave a disappointed grumble as he jogged to a stop in front of them.

Fessran took one sniff at him, then retreated, grimacing. "Herding teacher, you are wearing the most disgusting stink I have ever smelled on anyone."

"You'd better get used to smelling me this way." Thakur grinned. "Those duck-footed dapplebacks won't let me near them unless I roll in their dung. I'm sure there is plenty for you."

Fessran gave her ruff a disdainful lick, as if the noxious stuff was already on her. "I don't mind herdbeast dung, but I can tell these beasts don't eat grass. Ugh!"

"May you eat of the liver and sleep in the driest den," Ratha said, touching noses with him, but her whiskers twitched back. She rubbed her forehead against his cheek and started to slide along him, her tail crooked over, but she broke off midway, saying, "Fessran may be rude, but she's right. Phew, that's strong!"

Feeling like a pariah, he took a position downwind from both and asked them stiffly if that was better. Now that his own aroma was carried away by the breeze, he caught the maddening meat-smell and wondered where it was coming from.

Ratha had only her treeling on her back, but Fessran was festooned with something odd. It looked like she had rolled in some vines and had ended up tangled in strands and bundles of leaves.

Fessran turned abruptly to Ratha and said, "Well, we've carried the food long enough. Get your treeling to undo these leaves, and we'll feed Thakur before his tongue hangs out so far he steps on it."

At a nudge and purr from Ratha, Ratharee hopped onto Fessran's back and started pulling a leafy bundle apart. From the covering, Ratha drew a chunk of meat with her fangs and offered it to the herding teacher. Thakur didn't think about where it had come from; he just plopped down with the food between his paws and began slicing it with his side teeth. It was liver.

The richness of it soon sated him enough so his curiosity arose once again. He got to his feet, licking his chops, and asked how the two females had carried it.

Ratha showed him cords of twisted bark fiber that bound large leaves still covering the remaining bundles of food. He saw how the cords were wrapped about the Firekeeper's body to lash the packets to her sides.

"The leaves keep flies off," Ratha explained. "The meat isn't as good as we'd get from a cull, but it isn't carrion either."

Thakur sniffed a packet then turned to Ratha. "Did you think of this?"

"A Firekeeper student and his treeling came up with these twisted bark vines. You saw them being used to bind wood. Fessran figured out that we could use them to lash things onto ourselves, and since we knew you'd be hungry . . ."

"And we thought we'd be hungry too, after a while," Fessran reminded her. "Although I'm beginning to wonder if the idea was so clever. I'm not sure I'm ever going to get myself untangled from this mess."

Thakur stretched, enjoying his full stomach. One thing good about liver was that it was so rich that one didn't have to gorge oneself to feel sated.

"You can have more, Thakur," Fessran offered, evidently wanting to be rid of the sticky bundles against her sides. "After all, we did come to see your duck-footed dapplebacks, and the best way to start is to see how they taste. I imagine we'll have plenty of fresh meat, so there's no use saving this."

"I would save it anyway," Thakur answered carefully, trying not to show the sudden dismay he felt when he heard her words.

Ratha glanced at him curiously, and he knew she sensed his change in mood. He might be able to conceal his feelings from Fessran, since she often paid little attention to such things, but not Ratha.

She took him aside and said, "Thakur, have you found that these animals are not suited to our purpose after all? If that is true, I won't be angry. You did say you needed to study them before we arrived, and you have done so."

Thakur looked back at her, knowing she had grown well into her role as leader. "No, that is not what troubles me." With a wary glance at Fessran, he explained his concern that a Named invasion of the seamare herd might frighten away the young cripple who lived among the creatures. And too much disruption might cause the herd itself to flee from the jetty.

"It would be better for us to learn with just a few animals," he said. "There is a smaller group of duck-foots who make their homes in the rocks north of the jetty itself. If we work with those, we will do better."

Ratha agreed that his plan sounded wise and asked him to take her and Fessran to see the creatures. But first, she said, she wanted to see the spring. If the Named were to bring their herds here, she must be sure that there was forage and water to sustain them.

Slightly inland from the beach lay a scarp whose face was cut in a sheer cliff. A forest of mixed broadleaf and small pine grew in the cooling shadow thrown by the cliff. From cracks in slate and blue bands of rock, the water came, bearing the scent and taste of earthen caverns. It did not gush but ran in a steady, even stream without faltering.

"The smell of this water tells me it will never dry up," Ratha said, squinting up through the rich, slanting light between the trees. Thakur watched her crouch on a stone and dip her chin into the pool that collected beneath the spring. "The gravel bottom won't muddy when the herdbeasts drink. You have done well to find such a place."

Then she and Fessran began inspecting low-hanging boughs to be sure none of the new foliage could harm herdbeasts. Nosing through brush and grass, Thakur helped them search for poisonous weeds or plants with white berries. He also kept a lookout for an annoying herb with leaves that grew in clusters of three, which could cause the Named to itch if it got through to the skin beneath their fur or on their noses.

He walked with Ratha between thickets, looking at the quantity and freshness of the leaves, then wandered through the scattered clearings where grass grew, watered by seepage from the spring.

At last she gave a satisfied grunt. "This will be the clan's ground until the drought passes," she said finally. "Now, show me the animals."

Thakur led the two females behind the bluff overlooking the seamare terraces. He deliberately circled inland, giving the cliffs a wide berth so that the scents of his two companions would not betray their presence to Newt, who patrolled the rocks below.

He brought Ratha and Fessran to another, smaller headland area that overlooked a steep graveled beach. From an overlook above, he stretched out a paw toward the seamares.

Fessran wrinkled her nose at the sight of the creatures sprawled out all over the beach. "They don't look like much to me. Such lazy lumps. I like a creature with some spirit. And that smell is worse on them than on you."

"I think you will find they have spirit, especially when you try to taste their flesh," Thakur retorted.

Fessran wrinkled her nose again, but he ignored her. She wasn't the one who would decide.

"How would you keep these creatures?" Ratha asked.

"I would do as I saw the young stranger doing. I would gain their trust by defending their young from other meat eaters and take only those who have died."

"That will take much work and many days and provide only scraps while we do it. I think we should begin the way the first ones of the clan did with herdbeasts: catch and gather them in a place we can keep them."

"They must live in water," Thakur argued. "They will die if we drive them onto land and don't let them swim."

"Well, we certainly can't herd them on this beach. One sniff of us and splash—off they'd go." Ratha turned, scanning the landscape. "Look," she said, pointing with her muzzle. "There's another river emptying into this salty lake, and its waters look shallow. Perhaps we could keep the animals there."

They investigated the river mouth. Thakur judged the water salty enough for seamares, and holes on the muddy shore indicated the presence of the heavy-shelled clams on which the creatures fed. One channel in the river delta had made a deep meander into the side of a cliff, creating a crescent-shaped beach surrounded by sandstone walls on one side and the river on the other. The shallow and slowly flowing water allowed Ratha, Thakur, and Fessran to wade close to the center of the channel before their bellies even got wet.

"This is far enough from the waves so that the creatures

couldn't escape us," said Ratha. "And the cliffs trap them on all sides but one. It won't be easy, but we can keep them here."

Thakur agreed, although the thought of forcing the creatures to move from their graveled sea-beach bothered him a little.

The next task was to capture some seamares and move them. Thakur knew that the Named couldn't just go down on the beach, surround the creatures, and drive them alongshore to the river mouth. The beach was too narrow for the herders to maneuver, and the seamares could easily escape by diving into the breakers. But if one animal might be lured apart from the rest, the three could surround it.

The problem was how to lure the beasts. Thakur knew they ate large clams, but his efforts to dig one up and open it had so far failed. It was Fessran who pointed out that if the seamares ate such smelly things as fish, clams, and seaweed, they might be tempted by the meat she carried, which by now was also taking on an unmistakable odor.

To everyone's surprise, the idea worked. Using her treeling's dextrous paws, Ratha scattered a trail of meat fragments to lure a seamare into ambush. The first creature they captured was small and didn't put up much of a struggle. With three of the Named surrounding the beast, it humped and heaved itself from the graveled beach upriver to the site Ratha had chosen. The creature arrived, ruffled and blown, but in good enough shape to immediately start rooting in the mud for clams. Leaving Fessran to guard the first captive, Thakur and Ratha went back to bait the trail for another.

Soon a second, larger seamare started the trek to the river beach. This one gave the two herders more trouble.

"By the ticks on my belly, these duck-foots can move fast if they want to," Thakur yowled as he lunged to block the beast from wheeling and taking off back down the path.

"Watch the tusks," Ratha called over the seamare's outraged bellowing. An irritated jab just missed his hind-quarters as he skittered away.

"Yes, they're not as long as herdbeast horns, but they're down lower, where they can cause more trouble. Yarr, you stinking wave-wallower—go this way, not that!"

Soon there were more seamares than herders on the river beach. Thakur wanted to call a halt, but Ratha and Fessran had gotten excited. The bait was working well, and plenty remained. Both females had long since stopped complaining about the animals' fishy reek and were stalking and tricking the beasts with eager mischievousness.

Finally Thakur pointed out that if the Named collected too many more, they'd be spending too much effort chasing the creatures out of the river and trying to keep them from escaping back downstream. Reluctantly, Ratha agreed, for it was getting toward sunset. Thankfully, the sea-beasts slept by night, letting one of the three take each watch while the others slept.

The next day, Thakur found Ratha gone, while Fessran watched the seamare herd through sleep-reddened eyes. "How do I know where she's gone?" the Firekeeper growled irritably. "She said she was going to find some prickly bushes, and no, I don't have any idea why."

He found out when Ratha returned, her back laden with thornbrush, with Ratharee holding the branches on her. She also carried several rather gingerly in her mouth. Thakur could see the scratches on her muzzle.

"This may solve the problem of straying wave-wallowers," she said, dumping the brush and arranging it in a narrow heap as the Named did with firewood. Thakur could see that the prickly branches formed a low but effective barrier.

With his help, she fetched more brush and started to build a low wall. Thakur was dubious at first, but when he saw a seamare lumber up to the construction then retreat from the sharp thorns, he became convinced. They added thorny vines of wild blackberry, extending the barrier out toward the river.

Following Ratha's confident lead, he helped her build the wall into the lapping shallows. Then he saw her stop and stare in dismay as the gentle current stole every branch she had placed in the water, wafting them away.

She sat down, scratched herself in puzzlement. On her shoulder, Ratharee lifted her ringed tail in a questioning curve.

"Well, the branches need to be held down, somehow," Thakur began, but he was interrupted by a call from Fessran, who needed help to keep several seamares from humping themselves past her into the river.

Barrier building had to be abandoned for the moment, while the recalcitrant beasts were rounded up and driven back, but Thakur knew Ratha hadn't given up on the idea.

As soon as she could, she was back at it again. Fessran offered the suggestion that sticks pushed into the river bottom might serve to keep the thornbrush in place, and, after several tries, it worked. Not without cost, however.

Thakur had splinters in his pads and thornbark between his teeth by the time the two quit for the day.

Now that Ratha was assured that the spring Thakur found would serve the Named throughout the dry season, she decided to move the herds. She had considered the river where the seamares were kept as another possibility, but the outflow was so sparse that salt water had intruded, turning the river into a narrow arm of the sea. It was ideal for seamares but not other herdbeasts. The three-horns and dapplebacks would be moved to the area about the spring.

As soon as she told Fessran of her decision, the Fire-keeper wanted to leave, bearing the good news back to Cherfan and the others. After hearing Fessran grumble about "walking across all the rocks in the world," Ratha was surprised to see her so eager to make the journey once again.

Perhaps Fessran was starting to get restless, chafing at having to spend a good part of the day watching the captive seamares while Thakur and Ratha extended their brush wall into a corral that opened onto the river. Ratha had no doubt that Fessran would perform her task well and would take no nonsense from anyone. But she knew Fessran well enough to see that clan duty was not the only thing on the Firekeeper's mind.

After Fessran left, Ratha tackled the task of building a brush wall that would stand in the river's current. By ramming sticks into the mud-and-gravel bottom and having the treelings weave supple boughs between them, she and Thakur found that they could make a structure that held the seamares in while allowing water to pass through.

Ratha tried to adapt the method of lashing sticks together that the Firekeeper student had shown her, although it was difficult to get Ratharee to stop twisting bark strips into tangles once she had started.

As the wall slowly grew, with Thakur's help, Ratha wanted more seamares within the enclosure. When enough of the corral had been completed so that the beasts would not stray, she talked Thakur into another expedition to capture the beasts.

He was willing as long as they stayed north of the area where the Un-Named one prowled and did not take any that seemed to belong in that area. Another condition was that she disguise her smell by rolling in seamare dung. She grumbled, but she knew Thakur was right. She rolled.

They used the last of the smelly bait to lure more seamares and soon had as many as they could handle. The creatures milled about on the beach and sloshed in the water. Ratha and Thakur were kept busy reinforcing and raising the thornbrush walls.

When they weren't working on the seamare corral, Thakur showed her how to find things to eat in tidepools and how to glean the seamares' leavings. She did not like being a scavenger, even for a short while, and she was relieved when Fessran finally showed up at dawn one morning, along with Cherfan and Bira. She looked thin, dusty, but triumphant, leading a string of thirsty dapplebacks and three-horns, along with their equally thirsty herders.

Firekeepers arrived with the herders, bearing the Red Tongue in embers and on torches. Many of the Named looked tired and disgruntled at having to make the move, but no one growled or blamed Ratha, for they knew it was the drought that had forced them from their home ground.

Eagerly Ratha led them all to Thakur's spring, and she saw that the watering place would serve as well as she had hoped. Even with three-horns and dapplebacks milling and trampling, the flow stayed clear, and the animals drank until they were sated. Then the herders let them scatter to browse, and the rest of the Named sought dens or sleeping places nearby.

At last, when the confusion died down, she sought out Fessran. The Firekeeper was sitting on a rock ledge near the pool, grooming her belly and purring softly to herself. As Ratha approached, she caught something unusual in Fessran's smell, something sweet and almost milky. But the powerful seamare odor in her own coat interfered with her nose, and she couldn't tell if the odd scent was just her imagination. She consoled herself by thinking that Fessran would soon be wearing the odoriferous stuff and would smell as bad as she did now.

As she approached, Fessran stopped grooming and lay down. The elusive scent teasing Ratha's nose vanished as if it had never been. Fessran yawned, looking weary but happy. The strained look on her face seemed to have gone.

"Well, I did it." She grinned at Ratha. "I helped Cherfan whip that lazy bunch into shape and get them here."

"No one gave you trouble?"

Fessran licked some new scratches on her muzzle. "Oh, there were a few malcontents—there always are. I had to use a little persuasion, but not much. The sight of the dry streambeds helped change their minds." She shifted, grimacing and sneezing. "Would you mind sitting a bit farther away, clan leader? I mean no disrespect, but until I get used to that smell . . ."

Ratha moved herself, sitting a little apart, while Fessran told her how they had made the journey without losing a single fawn or foal. It suddenly struck her that the Firekeeper was preoccupied by something that had nothing to do with herdbeasts. She could tell by the absent tone in Fessran's voice and the way she groomed herself.

"Are you still thinking about your treeling?" she asked suddenly.

"What? Oh, Fessree? No. I'm sure she's surviving without me. No point in fretting, and I have other things to think about."

A little later Ratha paced away, swinging her tail. When she returned later to ask the Firekeeper something, she found Fessran gone.

She did not have much time to wonder where her friend had disappeared. No sooner had she turned away from the pool below the falls than she saw Thakur trotting up to her. She could tell by the way his whiskers bristled that this wasn't just a friendly call.

He jogged to a stop, Aree rocking on his back. Ratha lifted her chin, raised her whiskers.

"Ratha, I thought you told the herders not to take any wave-wallowers from the southern beach."

"I did," she said mildly.

"Well, they aren't obeying you," Thakur said. "I saw

several young herders bringing an animal over the rocks that separate our beach from the one Newt stalks."

Ratha's tail twitched with irritation. She did not like her instructions to be flouted, even though she had given them to appease Thakur. Privately, she didn't think that the Un-Named female Thakur called Newt would really miss a few wave-wallowers.

By the time the two backtracked to where Thakur had seen the stolen seamare and then made their way to the corral, the herding students were driving the beast past the brush wall. The herders, all yearlings, looked inordinately proud of themselves. Ratha thought sourly that the creature they had pirated was small and not really worth all the effort. She lost sight of the seamare as it lumbered past the thornbrush wall and mingled with the honking, hooting mass of its fellows.

She was about to tongue-lash the overenthusiastic youngsters when Thakur interrupted, asking if she had tracked the seamare through the brush gate and knew which one it was.

"No," she admitted, staring across the thornbrush at slick, mud-smeared flanks and swinging tusks. "I lost sight of the creature as soon as it got in."

Thakur sighed. "Newt isn't going to like this. I should have stopped those yearlings and returned the beast myself. I also don't know which others they may have taken."

"Does it really matter?" Ratha asked. "There are more on her beach than on ours. Surely she won't miss a few."

Thakur's ears twitched back. "Don't tell me you agree with what the herders did, Ratha!"

"I don't, and I was going to let them know that when

you stuck your whiskers in," she snapped. "Why is your nape all up about this anyway? Your lame friend has got more of the wave-wallowers than she needs."

"She knows them all, and she'll know if one is missing. She has favorites among them."

At this Ratha grimaced disdainfully.

"You may think it's silly, but she does," Thakur insisted. "She may tolerate us stealing a few, especially if she thinks they have wandered over from her beach, but if we take the wrong animal, we will have trouble. And I'm afraid we may have already done that."

"All right," Ratha said, seeing that he really was worried. "I'll tell everyone they'd better keep to our territory, or they'll have more than an Un-Named cripple to worry about."

She saw Thakur grimace at that and knew she should have chosen her words less recklessly. "I'm sorry, Thakur. She deserves more respect than that. I'll be sure the herders leave her alone."

She didn't like it when Thakur held her gaze with his own, his copper-furred face serious. "Don't underestimate Newt, Ratha."

Her tail did an irritated flip. Why was he getting so touchy about Newt, or whoever she was? Abruptly she decided to change the subject and asked him if he'd seen Fessran.

"I caught a glimpse of her going somewhere with Khushi," Thakur answered.

Ratha padded away. It seemed odd that Fessran was spending so much time with her son. None of the other Named females bothered much with their cubs once they were grown. She often had to scratch in her mind to remember who had birthed whom, on the rare occasions when it mattered. She shook herself and went on her way.

The following day, when she saw that the herdbeasts and the Named had settled after the journey, she gathered up those herders and Firekeepers who could be spared. After teaching them and their treelings how to work sticks and brush together to form a section of wall, she put them to work building the seamare pen.

Although Fessran still lacked a treeling, she made up for it by diligently bringing pieces of driftwood up from the beach and piling them near the wall.

Ratha had the pole-setters place additional sticks alongside the ones she and Thakur had laid. Once more poles were in place she worked alongside them with Ratharee on her back. The treeling held crossmembers where Ratha wanted them and helped to lash these in place. It was wearing work, hard on both Named jaws and treeling hands.

"Don't you think it's strong enough?" Fessran asked Ratha. "Watching you grunt and tussle in that miserable river is making me squirm."

From the shallow water where she was standing, Ratha eyed the wall and the seamares inside. "It needs more brush on top. I want to be sure those duck-footed belly-draggers can't escape."

"If you put more on top, it will fall over," Fessran argued, but Ratha wasn't in a mood to listen. She slogged her way out to midriver, where the construction crew and their treelings were reinforcing the barrier by shoving sticks and thornbrush into the crude latticework. Not satisfied with how the others were building the wall, she took a tangle of brush in her own mouth and clambered atop the construction.

"Here's where it should go," she said, and shoved the mass in the fork of a driftwood branch. As she stretched down to take more thornbrush that was being passed up to her, she felt the whole wall shift alarmingly under her weight. With squalls of dismay, the workers scattered as a section of the barrier toppled over, carrying Ratha and her treeling with it.

With a terrific splash, it fell into the river. Ratha expected a dunking but to her surprise, the woven mass of driftwood and brush held together, acting as a floating platform beneath her. Only her toes got soggy from water seeping through.

After getting over her initial shock, Ratha realized she was drifting downriver. She saw Fessran trotting along the bank, accompanied by several irritated pole-setters yowling insults at their reckless leader for knocking the wall down.

The current wasn't very strong, and soon Ratha's makeshift raft grounded on a sandbar. Everyone who wasn't occupied with keeping seamares from escaping waded in to steady the strange craft and rescue a frightened Ratharee, but Fessran and a few others took the opportunity to make sure Ratha got well splashed, dunked, and pummeled by the time she reached solid ground.

"Wait!" she yowled just as the Named were about to tear the raft apart to use in an attempt to repair the seamare pen. The group drew back, letting her through to examine the thing. She pushed on the craft with a paw, watching how it bobbed and floated. Again she clambered on, scrambling from one end to the other.

Yes, it made her feet soggy and had a disconcerting tendency to sink under her weight in certain places, but it had carried her quite a distance.

She hopped off, her whiskers bristling excitedly.

"I know that look," said Fessran. "Don't tell me you think we can use that broken piece of the wave-wallower pen."

"Didn't you see what happened? It carried me and Ratharee over the water. We didn't have to swim. I think it could carry more than one of us. Come on, Firekeeper. Let's both try."

Gingerly, Fessran made her way aboard, grimacing when Ratha joined her in a gleeful bound, making the raft bounce. "You, clan leader, are still a cub sometimes. Yarr, this thing makes my stomach feel queer."

"We can ride down the river on it," Ratha argued.

"*You* can ride down the river on it. I'll stick to burning my whiskers with the Red Tongue." Fessran disembarked, waded to the bank, and shook her feet. "Anyway, we need the sticks to fix the hole you made."

Reluctantly, Ratha gave up her new discovery, but as she watched the other Firekeepers pull it apart, she fixed the idea in her mind, resolving to build another raft once the pen was finished.

CHAPTER 9

THAKUR'S WORRY about Newt's reaction to the taking of her seamares by the Named soon proved true. Shortly after the incident with the two yearling herders, he learned that other herders had laid out bait trails to lure more seamares. But they had been scattered or trampled into the sand. There were reports that someone seemed to be hiding in the rocks, watching the herders, even if they stayed on their own beach. And one of the young herders who had been involved in the seamare stealing had been attacked by night. Though he was able to drive his assailant off, the ferocity of the attack frightened him. Thakur decided he had better find Newt.

He discovered her in the lagoon where she swam. When she saw him, her ears pricked forward, and she bounded out of the water. He saw, to his mixed delight and dismay, that her foreleg looked stronger and that she made attempts to use it, even on land. He felt a pang of guilt, wondering if his attempt to help her regain the use of her leg had led to her retaliation against the Named.

As soon as she had limped up to him and touched noses, he found she had worked on her speech as well as her leg. She greeted him with the words he had taught her. "Thakur come. Good. Newt swim with him?"

"No," he said carefully, "talk." In simple language he explained that the Named herders had been told to leave her and her seamares alone. In return, she was to keep to her territory. Any further ambushes would be looked upon with great disfavor by the leader of the Named.

"If there is another fight, and our clan leader knows I helped you heal your leg, there will be a bit of my fur flying as well," Thakur said.

"Fur fly," Newt echoed.

"I promise that no one will take any more of your seamares. If you do see Named herders on your ground, come and get me instead of fighting. You could get hurt."

Newt looked at the ground, growling. She made a noise like a seamare.

"No fights," Thakur said, "or we're both in trouble. My clan leader will stop me from helping you. Understand?"

She looked up at him and hissed a soft yes.

"Good. Now that's settled, what do you want to do?"

She hopped around him. "Teach. Words." Thakur grinned, unable to refuse her eagerness. She made a scrubbing motion with her good paw against her face. "Word," she said again.

"Wash," he said, licking a forepaw and performing the action. "I wash my face. You wash your face."

"Splash, wash, face place," Newt crowed.

Thakur flicked his tail. He didn't know what to make of her playful rhyming with sounds. He tried to recall if clan cubs did it. If so, they went through such a phase with their mothers before he got them to train.

"Stop being a pest and pay attention," he said severely.

"I'm washing my chest, see, like this." He tongued his ruff.

"Wash chest, best for pest," was her response.

He wondered where she had picked up some of the new words. Perhaps she had learned them from shadowing the Named herders, although not all the rhyming sounds she made had meaning. The fact that she had been able to pick up words and figure out their meanings indicated that her intelligence might be higher then he had first thought.

Even so, he wondered if anyone other than himself would understand her singsong garble. There was something oddly lyrical about the way she put sounds together.

He sighed. "You are strange."

"Strange, change, mange. Thakur talk, stalk. Newt swim," she said, and with an impatient toss of her head, she trotted back into the lagoon.

This time he did not join her but sat on a low dune overlooking the water and watched while she swam. Something had been plaguing him, and he decided that now was the time to sort it out. Ever since she had first spoken, the question had arisen within Thakur's mind: Had she come from the lineage of the Named?

Herding animals wasn't easy. Thakur knew how many of his own students, whose eyes were far brighter than Newt's, had struggled to learn how to judge a creature's mood or behavior. How could Newt think fast enough to outwit a beast?

She can plan, thought the herding teacher to himself. *She can think ahead and plan. I'm convinced of that.*

And the more he became convinced, the more a new certainty began to arise in his mind. *She has done this because she was born with the talent, ability, and need to manage other animals,* he decided. That conclusion could only lead to another: Somehow, this castoff from the ranks of the Un-Named had clan blood in her.

But how? Thakur thought of his own parentage, of his mother, Reshara, who took a male from outside. Such pairings were forbidden, and his mother was driven out. Hers was the last such mating until Shongshar's coming showed what a tragedy they could be.

No, Reshara was not the last clan female to dare an outside mating. Thakur sat up suddenly, his ears swiveling forward. Ratha and Bonechewer. She hadn't spoken much about it, but he remembered she had said something about having had cubs and having lost them. He'd assumed by her words that they had all died, but perhaps not.

Suppose one had survived, had somehow managed to scratch a living from the unfriendly world outside the clan. Without any of her own people to learn from, of course such a cub would be mute. But Newt looked too small to be a product of a mating several seasons past. Perhaps it was struggle and privation rather than age that had stunted her. And that crippling injury.

Everything was falling into place in Thakur's mind, but he knew that one piece of the picture still needed to be found, and that piece was in Ratha's keeping. His ears flattened slightly as he thought about asking her. Raising painful memories like that would not earn him favor. But if the outcast was indeed her daughter, the cub might well have talents needed by the clan. Especially now, when it appeared that Ratha would bear no cubs by any clan male.

He tried to argue himself into putting off questioning Ratha. But the more he pondered it, the more inevitable a confrontation seemed, and he knew it would grow larger and more intimidating the longer he waited.

With a sigh, he got up and went in search of Ratha.

He found Ratha on a high dune overlooking the river bend where the Named kept their seamares. She faced into the wind, her whiskers blown back along her muzzle. In her profile, etched against the sky, Thakur saw the same break in the line of forehead to nose that he had noticed in the outcast. A worry line creased the fur between her eyes as she stared down at the herders and their new charges.

Instead of questioning her about her cubs by Bone-chewer, he asked what was troubling her.

"Our duck-footed dapplebacks aren't doing as well as I expected. They just lie around in the mud all day or slosh in the river. We dig clams for them, but they won't eat very much."

"Perhaps this isn't the best place to keep them," Thakur answered.

"Maybe." Ratha looked away. "I keep a watch on that bunch of seamares on the jetty where your odd little friend stays. You know, you may be right about the way she manages them. Hers are doing better than ours." Her ears flicked back. "She may just have better stock."

"I don't think that makes much difference." Thakur chose his words carefully, not wanting Ratha to go back on her promise to leave Newt's seamares alone. "She doesn't so much manage the creatures as live with them. If we had patience, we could do the same."

Ratha's tail tip gave an annoyed twitch, then she yawned and stretched herself. "Dear herding teacher, you speak the truth even when you don't mean to," she said. "What you really meant is, if I had patience. And I don't, do I?"

Thakur decided not to make things more awkward by agreeing that patience was not one of her strengths. Instead he said, "I know that soon new cubs will be coming and you have to be sure there is food for the mothers." He paused. "This is one way." He indicated the penned seamares below with a downward jerk of his head.

"It will do for this season, but I'm not sure about the next," Ratha said moodily. "You know, Thakur, I keep thinking about that outcast. Where could she have come from? How can she do what she does if she is one of the witless Un-Named?"

Thakur said quietly, "Remember that not all those outside the clan lack the light in their eyes or the need to give themselves worth."

He could see that he had stirred some old memories. Her eyes went opaque for a few instants, as if she were turning inward. Their green became murky, turbid, reminding Thakur of the colors in Newt's. Perhaps the lame female's gaze was turned permanently inward, causing the cloudiness in her eyes.

"Ratha," he began, "I need to ask you something. You told me once that you had a litter by Bonechewer. I didn't ask you anything more about it, but now I must. Did any of those cubs live? Were any given names?"

Her upper lip quivered, jerked back, baring a fang. He saw a shiver pass along her sides. "I don't know," she said tonelessly. "He said . . . he said . . ."

Suddenly she whirled, almost pouncing on Thakur, her eyes bright with pain. "Why are you making me remember this? Wasn't it you who said let dead things be buried?"

"Are they dead, Ratha?"

She answered distantly, "I don't know. I fought with Bonechewer. He struck back. I told him he could keep the empty-eyed cubs he sired on me. Thistle-chaser got in the way. . . ."

Her voice grew faint as she began speaking not to him but to herself. Thakur's ears swiveled forward, straining to hear her better. "Who?" he asked.

Ratha was still off in the past. "It wasn't a real name," she said softly. "Not like the names we give ourselves in the clan. But I needed something to call her by. I hoped that she was something more than just a little beast wearing the skin of our kind." Her belly heaved as she tried to swallow her grief. "She was always jumping at thistles and getting thorns in her nose. She would never learn. Bonechewer didn't like it when I called her a thistle-chaser, but he never liked what I called him either."

"So that was her name? Thistle-chaser?"

"What does it matter?" Ratha's fangs flashed again in anger as she spoke. "Names are for those who know what names mean. My cubs didn't and never will." She was trembling now.

Thakur rubbed his cheek against her. "I'm sorry, Ratha. I didn't know how much it would hurt you to remember. Leave it behind."

"I didn't claw Bonechewer because he lied to me," she

said. "He just didn't tell me the truth. And in the fight . . . she got in the way. . . ."

Thakur put more firmness into his voice. "Leave it behind, clan leader. You have other things to think of now."

She gave a weak grin. "Such as lazy lumps in the mud and other people's cubs, I suppose. All right, herding teacher, you don't have to look so worried. I'm all right now."

Thakur caught himself. He had been thinking hard, but not about Ratha as she stood here before him now. His mind was on the story she had told him. When she realized the truth about her cubs, she must have turned on Bonechewer in a savage, bitter fight.

And the words she had said repeated themselves in his own mind: "She got in the way." Then what had happened? Was the cub struck or bitten, perhaps more severely than Ratha intended? Enough to cripple and stunt the young body?

Ratha was staring at him with an odd look on her face. "I can also put footprints together into a trail, Thakur. You are thinking that odd outcast who lives with the seamares might be my cub. Well, that's impossible, because she's clearly a cub born in the last birthing season. If Thistle . . . if my daughter had lived, she would be several seasons old by now."

The herding teacher knew better than to try arguing. Ratha had a stubborn set to her jaw and a tang to her smell that told him she had made her decision, reasonable or not, and would not be budged.

This bothered him a little. When Ratha was this obstinate, she usually had a good reason. But this felt more as if she were fighting because she was afraid, because she feared the outcast might be the daughter she had abused and abandoned.

He suppressed his impulse to ask her more questions and turned away, leaving her staring out over the beach. He had gotten what he came for. Not only did he know more about Ratha's split from Bonechewer, but he now knew the name of the female cub. Though, as Ratha said, it wasn't a real name, perhaps it had been used enough so that the cub might remember what the word sounded like, if not its meaning.

He said the name softly to himself when he was far enough away to be beyond Ratha's hearing. *Thistle-chaser*.

CHAPTER 10

RATHA TRIED to bury the feelings that Thakur had raised by indulging in something she had wanted to do ever since the section of wall had fallen into the river and transformed itself into a raft. The following day she turned over the seamare-watching duties to other herders and went off by herself with Ratharee on her shoulder.

Again she gathered sticks, bark, and brush. The task was easier this time, for she didn't need to use thornwood. Ratharee was eager to show her skills once again, and soon the two were well launched on their project.

At the end of the day, Ratha hid her materials and the beginnings of her raft and returned to her clan-leader duties. But things seemed well enough settled that she could afford some time to herself, and she took advantage of the lull.

The following afternoon, Ratha crouched with her head bent over Ratharee's back as the treeling wove the sticks and brush together with twisted bark cord. The raft was half-finished when she caught the scent of seamare mixed with that of the clan's herding teacher.

She stood up as Thakur came forward with Aree on his back. Half-embarrassed, half-proud, she showed him what she and Ratharee had made. She couldn't help a backward flick of her ears and hoped he wasn't going to question her again about her lost cubs.

He said nothing about them. Instead, he circled the half-built raft, eying it judiciously.

"You might try adding some bundles of dry reeds near the water," he suggested, and offered to go collect them. Ratha, suspecting that the offer was an apology of sorts for upsetting her, readily agreed, and after that the two spent all the time they could spare at the task. Sometimes, Ratha noticed, Thakur didn't come, or he would arrive late from an unexpected direction, reeking of seamare. Not wanting to ask or answer any questions, she made him work downwind of her until finally the raft was finished.

Triumphantly she dragged it from the construction site to the brackish estuary. With Thakur and the tree-lings helping, she got the raft floating. As he steadied it, with Aree riding nervously on his shoulder just above the waterline, Ratha and her treeling clambered aboard.

The craft floated, but it rocked alarmingly, and she found herself shifting her feet continually to keep from tipping. When Thakur released the raft, it did tip, spilling both her and Ratharee off into the shallow water.

"It's too narrow," she said mournfully, after enduring an excited scolding from Ratharee. She licked herself and the treeling, trying to press the water from both soggy coats.

Widening the raft and giving it more support in the form of bundled-reed outriggers helped solve the tipping problem, but Ratha soon found there was something else she had overlooked: She had no way to control the thing, to make it go where she wanted.

After riding weak but malicious currents to disaster several times in a row, she hauled her drenched self and her recalcitrant boat ashore and glared at it. Ratharee, who had abandoned her for Thakur in the interests of staying dry, made an insincere attempt to comfort her and backed away from the water streaming from her coat.

Irritably, she shook herself, growling that she should have known better than to waste effort on such a useless thing.

"It isn't that useless," Thakur observed. "It does keep you out of the water when you walk on it." He added that if she tethered her raft to shore at both ends in a narrow part of the river, the Named wouldn't have to wade or swim to get across.

That idea mollified Ratha somewhat. Instead of wrathfully shredding her treacherous construction, she followed

Thakur's advice, tethering her raft among the reeds at a narrow spot, where it served as a floating footbridge.

Having satisfied her urge for raft building, Ratha devoted her attention once more to things that had begun to worry her. One of these was the Firekeeper leader.

Ratha thought at first that Fessran was keeping away from her and Thakur because of the seamare smell they wore. Fessran balked at taking on the same scent. She pointed out that her work ruined her odor enough with the harsh stink of ash. And, as Firekeeper, she didn't have much to do with seamares once the herders had settled into their duties.

Ratha accepted that. Those of the Named who had adopted the practice of disguising their scents had done so willingly. They saw the advantage when Thakur showed that it made the wave-wallowers less restive. But she didn't want to force anyone into it; scents were strongly personal issues among the Named, and some had more sensitive noses than others.

So Fessran remained free of the seamare stink and avoided those who had it. But Ratha noticed that she seemed to sit at a greater distance from her than from Thakur. And that whenever Ratha approached, she would stop grooming her belly and immediately switch to washing her face.

Ratha knew that not all of the Firekeeper's coolness to her was due to her smell. The forced abandonment of the Un-Named litterling still rankled; there was resentment in Fessran's eyes, even though the Firekeeper had said she didn't care.

It was late in the summer and a hot day, even on the sea coast. The herdbeasts sought shade in the forest, and the seamares wallowed in the shallows enclosed by part of their corral. With heat making the animals lazy, the herders too could relax. Ratha decided to take a break from overseeing the seamare herders and went to drink from the pool beneath the spring.

Coolness from the spring seemed to blow away the heavy, hot air surrounding her as she came down the deeply shaded path. Spray-moistened moss cushioned her feet when she crouched to drink. She lapped her fill, then laid first one side of her face, then the other, in the pool, letting the chill seep through her fur. As she dangled a forepaw in the water, she glanced up to the rock ledges above, wondering which one would be best for a nap.

One ledge was already taken. Sandy fur showed against blue-tinted stone. Fessran was there, relaxing and starting to groom herself. One rear leg stuck stiffly over her head as she began licking the creamy fur on her belly.

The soft chuckle of the stream had covered Ratha's footsteps, and the wind blew her scent away. Fessran didn't know she was here. The idea of spying on the Firekeeper made Ratha uncomfortable, and she was about to announce herself when something disquieting about Fessran's grooming caught her attention.

Slowly she backed under a hanging bunch of ferns, shielding herself from Fessran's view. Absently she licked the back of her own forepaw and began to scrub her cheek, wondering what it was about Fessran's grooming that disturbed her. And then, aware of the motion of her own forepaw over her face, she froze, knowing she had found her answer.

When Ratha groomed, she always started by scrubbing her cheek with the side of her forepaw. So did the others of the Named. Only if a Named female was pregnant or nursing did she break the inborn pattern and start by grooming her stomach. Ratha peeked out from beneath the ferns. Fessran wasn't carrying cubs. She hadn't come into heat this year. But she could be nursing.

A Named female could give milk without birthing a litter. If a female took in a motherless orphan, the cub's suckling could make her produce milk in a matter of days—even sooner if she badly wanted to feed the litterling. And Fessran had wanted to.

Ratha watched Fessran lick and nibble, taking great care over her belly. She felt a slow anger start to burn away the refreshing coolness from the pool. Yes, Fessran must be nursing. She had kept the cub, despite the orders to Khushi that the litterling be returned. Ratha crouched beneath the ferns, feeling hot-and-cold surges of anger and betrayal. What a fool she had been!

Her first mistake had been letting Fessran go with Khushi. She imagined how the Firekeeper must have persuaded the young herder not to obey the clan leader's orders and instead to turn the cub over to her. And then the two had stayed away to make it look as though they had made the journey. It must have been then that Fessran found she could suckle the orphan.

Ratha ground her back teeth. She could see them now in her imagination, Fessran lying in the shade, nursing the Un-Named cub. Such a sweet maternal scene it must have been! And Khushi, sitting by, looking torn and bewildered because he had not wanted to disobey Ratha's orders.

But well-chosen words from his mother about the value of a cub's life and the sorry blindness of a clan leader might well have swayed him. Fessran, she remembered, was very good at choosing words.

So they had kept the Un-Named orphan, the two conspirators, and even brought him along when the herds moved from the old clan territory to the coast. No wonder Fessran had been so itchy to return from the first expedition.

And I saw all of that, but I chose to look the other way. Now they're shoving my nose in it.

She repressed an urge to bound up from ledge to ledge until she reached the one where Fessran sat. That would do no good and might lead to embarrassment or worse, should her sense of balance be overwhelmed by her sense of outrage. Instead she came out from beneath the ferns and called Fessran down. After a few grumbles, the Firekeeper came.

Ratha sat, looking at the ripples that spread from the cascading of the falls into the pool. Fessran sat down a short distance away from her. Deliberately, Ratha said nothing until the Firekeeper started to fidget.

"Am I keeping you from your grooming?" Ratha asked. "Please continue. I'm just nursing my thoughts."

With a sidelong look at her, Fessran wet a paw and slowly started massaging her cheek.

"Shouldn't you start with the fur on your belly?" Ratha made her tone more pointed.

"Ratha, what are you talking about? If you have something to tell me, just say it and quit chasing your tail." Fessran's own tail switched irritably.

Ratha got up and paced toward her, keeping her eyes fixed on Fessran's. "You know what I'm talking about: keeping your teats clean to nurse a cub. That Un-Named litterling I made Khushi return never was taken back to the place he was found, was he?" She felt the hackles on her neck rising. "You may be keeping your teats clean, Firekeeper, but the rest of you stinks, and the smell is worse than the seamare dung on me."

Fessran's face grew tight as her ears flattened. "All right. Yes, I kept Mishanti."

"Mishanti? By the Red Tongue's ashes, you've already given him a name?"

"Yes, because he deserves one. You are wrong about him, Ratha. As soon as Khushi stopped for a rest, I looked at that cub, and I knew that if we took him out and abandoned him, I would hate myself for the rest of my life. It would be like killing one of my own litter."

Ratha closed her eyes. "We've trodden this path already, Fessran. You know where it leads. I thought when you turned from me to support Shongshar and his fire-dance, it was something that would happen only once. Now you have disobeyed me again, tricked me, lied to me."

Fessran swallowed and her laid-back ears began to droop, but the determined glitter stayed in her eyes. "The part of you I disobeyed and tricked and lied to," she said slowly, "is not the part of Ratha that I know. The part I know would not have me kill or abandon this cub out of a fear of what he might become."

Ratha gritted her teeth. "You forget too easily. Shongshar . . ."

"Stop holding Shongshar over my head," Fessran hissed. "This isn't the same at all. A cub's life is what I seek, not power over the Named."

"What *is* the same is a headstrong Firekeeper who does what her belly tells her without regard for what anyone thinks, even me."

This stung. Ratha could see Fessran flinch. "You don't think I didn't worry about your feelings? I'll tell you, I spent a lot of time thinking."

"With that misbegotten Un-Named suckling curled up next to you, kneading your belly," Ratha sneered.

Fessran's voice and eyes went cold, stabbing Ratha deeper than she expected. "You are wrong about Mishanti, clan leader. You don't know how wrong."

Ratha turned away from her, began to pace the banks of the pool. She stopped to look at herself, saw the bared teeth, the angry eyes that did not look quite like hers. Was Fessran right? What part of her was saying these ugly things? And was there something blinding her to what Fessran saw?

She made an angry turn, tore up moss with her claws as she pivoted. When she came back to Fessran, she had trodden down her doubts and felt as cold and determined as the Firekeeper looked.

"Fessran, I won't exile you from the clan, as I have the right to. I need you too badly. I also know that you don't have the skills to survive outside."

At this, Fessran bridled, but Ratha could see she knew the truth of those words. Fessran had managed her own stays away from the clan only by depending on the hunting and fishing skills of others.

"I will, however, break you down in rank to the lowest

wood-stacker and give you a few good swipes into the bargain if you don't get rid of that cub. And if I come and find him in your den, I'm taking him. Is that clear?"

Fessran's sides heaved. She looked at the ground. "It is, clan leader. And I am very sorry for you."

"If you're sorry for me, don't hurt me any more. Do what I told you to in the first place." Ratha turned and left, without waiting to see what Fessran's reaction would be.

Thakur watched Newt's foreleg sweep back and forth beneath the water of the lagoon. She could move it fast enough now to make a little wave curl over her paw.

"Stronger?" Newt asked.

"Much stronger," Thakur answered. "Good. You've been working."

"Swim. Out there." Newt jerked her muzzle toward the ocean. "Helps."

"Now let's try stretching again," Thakur said, wading out of the pool toward a heavy driftwood log. "See if you can keep your claws fastened in the wood and then pull so your muscles stretch." He watched as Newt emerged, still limping, but no longer holding her foreleg against her chest. Now her foot brushed the ground, and Thakur hoped she might soon be able to put some weight on it.

She did the exercise as he directed, getting a clawhold in the gray driftwood and pulling back with all her weight to limber and stretch the contracted muscles. He saw Newt grimace as she pulled hard, straightening her leg.

"Hurts," she said between grunts of effort. "But good for leg."

Then Thakur saw her abruptly freeze, her claws still

embedded in the log, her stare fixed at a point beyond. Even as his gaze followed, his nose caught the smoke-tinged scent of the Firekeeper leader. Beside him, he felt Newt tense, jerk her claws from the driftwood, and start to growl.

Fessran sat in a hollow between two dunes, cocking her head to one side. "Phew, herding teacher," she said, wrinkling her nose. "I had to force myself to follow your trail. You don't have to roll in seamare dung now that we've got the creatures penned." She got to her feet, her eyes roving over Newt. "And who is that? She stinks as much as you do."

Thakur didn't know whether Newt understood Fessran or not, but he heard her growl deepen. "No," he said sharply, pushing Newt back with his shoulder.

"So I'm not the only one who has dealings with the Un-Named." Fessran grinned. "What does our clan leader have to say about this?"

"If Ratha has anything to say about it, you can be sure she will," he said irritably.

Fessran fixed her gaze on Newt, who bristled. "When did she turn up?"

"She's the one who gave me the idea about herding seamares." Thakur turned to Newt. "Put your fur down," he told her. "That is Fessran. She's often rude, but she won't harm you." He halted. Newt's eyes had gone glassy and started to swirl.

"The smell," he heard her hiss. "In her coat. The Dreambiter's smell."

Before Thakur could stop Newt, she was over the log in a bound and charging at Fessran. The puzzled stare on the Firekeeper's face turned to an angry snarl. Thakur sprinted after Newt, trying to launch himself between the two, but he wasn't fast enough. Newt and Fessran met in an angry flurry, then broke apart. Newt suddenly withdrew, muttering to herself. Fessran stood, her head lowered, her nape erect, ready to fight off another attack, but Newt had gone into a strange trance in which she circled aimlessly for several minutes, looking confused, then toppled over onto her side.

"What, by the Red Tongue's ashes, is the matter with *her*?" Fessran demanded.

Thakur lost his temper. "What is the matter with *you*, Firekeeper? I told the others I didn't want to be disturbed, but you obviously didn't listen."

"I'm sorry, Thakur," Fessran said contritely. She flattened her fur, came a few steps closer. "Is she all right?"

"Her name is Newt, and she's not going to die, if that's what you mean. But she's not all right. She gets these fits. Her foreleg is injured, and I was trying to help her when you stuck your whiskers in."

"What was she saying about my smell?"

"I don't know. I think your scent had something to do with the fit. Maybe you'd better back off." Thakur nosed the fallen Newt, who had started to twitch and stir. Fessran retreated downwind as Newt slowly rolled onto her front and shakily got up. "Just because I don't cover myself with duck-footed dappleback dung . . ." Thakur heard the Firekeeper mutter. Newt shook her head in confusion then peered at Fessran. For an instant, he thought she was going to attack again. Then she took a breath and spoke.

"You," she said hoarsely to Fessran. "You carry smell. You not biting one, but you carry smell."

"What's she yowling about?" Fessran asked.

"I don't know. Fess, just go away, please."

Newt startled him with a roar. "No! Stay. Tell about smell." She turned almost desperately to Thakur, stumbling badly on her words. "The one who bites. In my head. Smell is real. Newt didn't make up." She lunged away from Thakur, facing Fessran. Then she seemed to catch sight of the scars on Fessran's leg and chest. She looked up, searching Fessran's eyes.

"Not only smell, but scars," she breathed. "Like me."

Caught in the intensity of Newt's gaze, Fessran twitched back her ears and narrowed her eyes.

"You know Dreambiter," Newt insisted stubbornly, unwilling to release Fessran from her stare.

"I have many scents on me, from all those in the clan," Fessran answered cautiously. "Who do you mean by *Dreambiter?*"

"She comes. From behind, in darkness. I hear her feet, then she leaps on me and wounds me with teeth. I remember taste of milk, sound of purring, but then came pain and this." Newt thrust her lame forepaw at Fessran.

Thakur tried again to ease himself into the conversation, but the two were intent upon each other and took no notice of him.

"Newt, who was your mother?" Fessran asked.

She got only a blank stare.

"Mother. You know, the one who birthed you, gave you milk."

"The Dreambiter gave me milk." Newt's voice was flat. "I don't know *mother.* Does *mother* bite?"

"A little nip once in a while, if cubs are being rowdy. But mostly she feeds them, keeps them warm, gives them nuzzles and licks. I've had young ones myself, so I know." Fessran gave her a quizzical look.

Thakur saw that Newt was retreating into her memories, muttering to herself. He saw the link she was forging between Fessran's description of a mother and the Dreambiter image that plagued and terrified her.

"The one who bit me is the one you call *mother*, and she is in your clan." Newt's ears flattened slightly, and her pupils widened with fear then narrowed with rage. Thakur felt a stab of alarm.

"Who in the clan could . . ." Fessran broke off. Thakur saw her mouth a name to herself and felt it tremble on his own tongue: Ratha.

"Enough, Fessran," he said sharply, wishing he'd stepped in before things got this far. Newt was starting to shiver and growl.

The Firekeeper bristled. "Why shouldn't I tell her the truth? If this cub is from the loins of our clan leader, then Ratha has no right to judge others."

"I don't think it will help us or her to dig up old and rotted dung," Thakur snapped. "Firekeeper, if you are going to cause trouble, do it somewhere else."

Fessran left, her tail low and switching. Thakur didn't like the way Newt's gaze followed her.

Newt extended her patrol range and hobbled along her new trails with raised nape and bristling tail. Now that she had gone beyond her own beach, she caught the scents of the intruders in the wind and found a trace of the Dreambiter's among them. It made her shudder—and fight off rising panic that threatened to tip her over into an attack of her strange illness.

The gentle one who called himself Thakur had not come since that meeting with the other female, the one who carried the scent of the Dreambiter. After that encounter, he refused to answer Newt's questions and at last had turned away, saying he should no longer visit her.

She found herself missing Thakur with a keenness that added to her misery. Why had he come if he meant only to go away again? Why had he tempted her to speak if there was no one to hear her and answer?

She thought of becoming silent once again, but she found that she couldn't. It seemed as if the words were jammed up behind her tongue, pushing to get out, yet she didn't know how to say them. Something had changed in her. He had done it.

Her rage made her reckless, and she followed the scents of the Named until she found herself crouched in the lee side of a dune, looking down at a strange sight.

She had come to another river resembling the one that formed her lagoon. This stream meandered its way across sand flats that lay at the base of a sandstone cliff. At one point the cliff was gouged inward, forming a pocket, and there, on the narrow mud-beach beneath the cliff, Newt saw a cluster of seamares.

She stifled her impulse to go and herd them back to the rookery, for the Named invaders on both sides of the river guarded the captives. From this distance, she couldn't tell if any of the sentries was the Dreambiter.

When she crept closer for a better view, she saw something going on that she didn't understand. The intruders were doing something she had never seen any animal do:

carrying long sticks in their jaws and poking them upright into the mud on the seamares' beach.

A line of poles already extended down the beach into the water, and as she watched, two of the Named waded out with saplings from which the branches had been stripped and shoved them into the sandy bottom, continuing the line of upright sticks in the river itself.

As the pole-setters worked, forcing the sticks into place with their jaws, another group followed them. This bunch carried odd little animals on their backs. Newt remembered the creature Thakur always carried with him. The ringed tails, strange paws, and sharp little muzzles were the same.

She watched as the intruders brought shorter sticks in their jaws and held them crossways against the uprights. The other animals reared up and did something with their paws and long pieces of vine that then held the crossmembers in place. When they finished each section, Newt saw what they had built. It was like a tree, but not a tree, or like a bush that had been wrenched and bent to serve some unknown purpose. Bewildered and frightened, she crept away.

The next day found her back behind the dunes, spying on the strangers. She could see that the mysterious thing had grown, now extending from the mud-beach to mid-river, then bending at an angle to follow the current flow downstream.

She still didn't know what it was, but as the strangers and their small helpers continued to put poles in place and lash them together, she gained a dim sense of what this thing might be. Then, when the builders brought tangles of thornbrush and added those to the construction (not without grimaces of pain and yowls when tender noses got pricked), she began to understand. She watched a seamare lumber up to the construction, hoping the creature might butt it down. Instead the animal nosed it, then bellowed as the thorns stung its muzzle. It retreated, beaten and bewildered, and made no other attempt to escape.

Now Newt understood. This thing was a barrier, an obstruction, like a wall of rock or tangled, thorny growth. It shocked and dismayed her that anyone would make something like this. She growled deep in her throat as she watched the barrier grow, encircling the apprehensive seamares.

She thought of Thakur and her promise that she would come to him instead of launching an attack on the Named. But the thought of Thakur only made her angrier. He was one of those invading strangers who had captured the seamares; he would do nothing to help.

She was weary from all the thinking she had done. As the afternoon shadows lengthened, she tried and failed to come up with a way to free the seamares. At last she sank into the wordless, dull anger of defeat.

The barrier was nearly completed. The seamares huddled in the center, bewildered and miserable. From her vantage point, Newt could see that the barrier enclosed most of the mud-beach and ran out into the river, giving the creatures only limited room to swim. She remembered swimming with Splayfoot and seeing the seamare fly through the twilight under the ocean. These strangers had no understanding of the seamares, and they didn't care. She sniffed the scents coming to her on the wind.

There was already the taint of sickness in the odors of the trapped creatures.

Shifting restlessly, she raked the dune. Sand ground under her claws. And then she watched again, this time fixing her gaze on the intruders themselves as they worked to set the last stakes in place before bundling them with thorns. She saw how the cats struggled, often getting splinters in their jaws and blunting their fangs while bringing heavy sticks to midriver and setting them in place. Sometimes they set a pole wrong, or a surge of current from the stream pushed the stake over.

Often she saw two or three of the strangers, coats muddy and soggy, hanging on to a pole with their claws and trying to sink the end deep into the mud bottom by their combined weight. Half the time the stake sagged when they released it, then came loose and was carried downstream. Growling with frustration, the workers retrieved it and fought to anchor it in place again.

It was not a task for which they were well suited, and that became more obvious the longer Newt watched them work. Yet, although she disliked what they were doing, she could not help seeing how hard they tried. It reminded her of her own struggles, and she saw a tiny bit of herself in the strangers. She could also see that, despite the difficulty, they were succeeding.

She stayed until evening, hoping to creep closer by dark. When she approached the seamares' pen, she found that the night she hoped would shield her had been pushed back. On the banks of the river were strange bright spots she had never seen before. They flickered and danced, like reflections of the sun on the surface of her lagoon, and they cast a fierce light. Newt's nape prickled in terror. Were the invaders so powerful that they could capture pieces of the sun and hold them, as they did the seamares?

Though she trembled and wished she could retreat to the beach, with its soft darkness and swish of waves, she forced herself on. When she drew closer, the bright points took on form. To her they were a nest of yellow and orange snakes writhing together toward the night sky, hissing and snapping their jaws as if the stars were prey.

Beside the fires, outlined by the fierce light, she saw the forms of sentinels. In their eyes, even at a distance, the orange light shone in glints of amber and green.

The smell was harsh and choking, as irritating to her nose as the light was to her night-widened eyes. She shuddered. Here was a foe she could not face down, for the fear it struck in her lay too deep. She took flight back into the darkness and crouched on cold sand, watching and hating those glowing, writhing nests of snakes.

The acrid smell of smoke could not drown out the scents of the seamares behind the barrier. They still reached her and somehow reproached her for turning back. She kneaded the sand fiercely with her claws, drawn on by the seamare odor and pushed back by the ashes and smoke. At last she crept forward again. The snake-nests lay on both banks of the river, but there were no dismaying lights in the river itself. It lay open to her, a dark, safe path.

Wet sand felt clammy against her pads as she limped across the flats toward the river. She waded into the shallows, the night-chilled water seeping through the fur of her legs, her belly, and her flanks. Feeling ahead with her good forepaw, she sought the bottom drop-off that would show her the channel. The only way to conceal her approach was to swim underwater in the deepest part of the river.

After poking her nose up to take a breath, Newt slipped beneath the surface and down into the main channel. Here it was deep and wide enough for her to swim. The incoming tide overcame the downstream current, helping her to glide upriver, near the channel bottom. And the strange lights unexpectedly aided her by casting a glow into the murky gloom, so she could see her way ahead.

Each time she surfaced to breathe, she made herself inhale slowly and quietly rather than gulping air. The sentries stood with their faces turned outward, away from her. No one had seen or smelled . . . yet.

Gradually she worked her way upriver toward the mud-beach where the seamare pen had been built. Lifting her dripping head, she stared at the barrier of poles and thorns that now rose out of the water only a few tail lengths away. Those who had made it had unwittingly aided her by extending it into midriver, where the water was deep enough to conceal her.

She floated at an angle, with only her nose above the ripples, gathering breath and strength. Then she dived and shot toward the barrier, her good foreleg stretched out with claws extended. She hit the barrier hard underwater, ignoring the thorns that sank into her paw. Pulling thorn-tangles aside, she ripped away lashed cross-pieces, using her jaws to aid her good foreleg.

Sounds from the beach made her halt her destructive flurry and duck back into the depths of the channel. She hid there until her lungs were nearly bursting, expecting to hear angry roars and the noise of running feet, but nothing happened. Perhaps the noise she had made sounded loud only to her. Gasping, she surfaced, approached the barrier, and saw a horselike head rise from the water on the other side. Another followed, blowing quietly. The seamares knew what she was doing.

Feeling a sudden surge of triumph, she attacked the thorns and stakes again. One pole tipped sideways under her weight. She wrenched the lashings off another and pulled prickly branches aside, even though they stung her mouth and scraped her teeth.

She worked until she had cleared a narrow opening, then fought to widen it. Abruptly she heard a grunt and was nearly ploughed underwater when a heavy body rammed itself through the break. Another followed, and then another, as the seamares poured through. They churned the water into froth, bumped and banged her, but in her delight at having freed them, she didn't care.

Abruptly, yowls and sounds of galloping feet began from the shore. Newt saw sentinels running along the bank, some bearing branches with the writhing snakes of light curling about their ends. Fear quickly chilled her triumph. She sought the channel depths once more, stroking and kicking hard to keep up with the escaping seamares, whose wake helped to carry her along.

It seemed to take the Named intruders a long time to realize that the attack had come from the water. They were still dashing up and down the riverbanks by the time Newt and the seamares passed the last of their beacons and had swum far enough downstream so that night could shield their escape.

Gradually the noise and confusion died into the distance, as Newt and the seamares made their way back down the loops and meanders of the river toward the sea. The honks and grunts of her big companions blended into the wash of surf in a boisterous song of freedom.

The escapees hauled themselves out onto the night-silvered gravel of the beach, with Newt doing a three-limbed frolic around them. And when they reached the jetty and were gathered once more into the herd, Newt gamboled off to her sleeping place, wet and weary but happy.

CHAPTER 11

THOUGH THAKUR could see well enough in the early-morning dark to tell that the seamare pen was damaged, he had to wait until dawn to tell how badly. As the sun cast its first light over the salt fens near the estuary where the pen had been built, Thakur saw Ratha striding toward him, her shadow thrown far ahead of her and her form backlit by the dawn.

At first she stepped daintily, avoiding soggy patches or stopping to shake mud off her feet. But as the ooze deepened, she gave up and slogged through it to meet him. Wading into the chill water of the estuary, he showed her how one wall of the pen had been ripped open to free the seamares. Newt had not been content with just tearing an exit but had vented her wrath on the stick-and-lash construction, wrecking an entire section of wall where it stood in the deepest water.

Ratha sniffed a pole that had been knocked askew. Thakur could tell by her expression that she couldn't smell anything; the briny water had washed away any remaining odor. But he didn't need the odor to know who had done this and why. He also felt the sharp jabs of his conscience. He had helped and encouraged Newt to regain some use of her leg and with it increased mobility and a greater capacity to destroy what the Named had built. Still, the healer in Thakur argued, he had done the right thing.

"This was done by someone who could swim well, since the water was high last night," Ratha said. "Also someone who has plagued our efforts with the seamares ever since we arrived. And we both know who that is, herding teacher."

Thakur felt his ears and whiskers sag as water dribbled off them. "I didn't think she was strong enough to wreck the pen."

"That was a lot of work for us and the treelings," Ratha said. "And we are going to have to catch all the seamares again, which will be twice as hard. We may not be able to find them again." She paused. "Thakur, I've tried to be nice to you about this, but this three-legged renegade of yours has caused more trouble than we can afford right now. If I catch sight of her, I am going to give her a good cuffing to drive her away, and I'm ordering everyone else to do the same. Including you."

Thakur looked away. "You don't have to make that an order, clan leader," he growled between his teeth. "I know where my duty lies." Though he was furious with Newt, the thought of chasing her off only made him feel worse. He hung his head. "Ratha, the way we were keeping the seamares penned here wasn't a good thing. She tried to tell us in the best way she knew, and we didn't listen."

"By the Red Tongue's ashes, how are we supposed to keep the beasts where we want them, then? If we didn't pen them, they'd use those duck-feet of theirs to swim away, and then where would we be?" Ratha's teeth clicked as she shivered, and Thakur knew the chilly water wasn't doing her temper any good.

"The ones she keeps don't swim away," he retorted.

"But we can't live among them and just scavenge off dead young ones, as she does. Even in this small group, there are too many of us."

"Newt doesn't just scavenge. It's something more than that. She knows the beasts, and they know her. They accept her, and they trust her."

Ratha only snorted.

"No, it is true. Our herdbeasts may tolerate us and accept the protection we give them from other meat eaters, but we do not have the kind of bond that she seems to have developed with these seamares. That is what I want to learn from her."

"Is that worth a wrecked pen and so much work gone to waste?" she retorted.

Thakur was prepared to snap back at her when he realized how silly it must seem to anyone watching. Here stood the clan leader and the herding teacher, up to their bellies in clammy seawater, shivering and arguing.

"Come on, Ratha. Let's get out and fluff our coats dry, then we can talk sense," he suggested. He turned and splashed toward shore.

She followed, complaining that this soggy existence was going to ruin her coat. The salt crystals, she said, were already making her skin itch.

"Well, maybe the water will drown your fleas," he answered.

"That may be true. I don't have as many now," she admitted, her mood lightening as the morning sun warmed both of them. "Herding teacher, I understand that you think this outcast has something we should learn. I won't disagree with you, but"—and here she pointed her nose toward the pen—"I can't let something like this happen again. Keep her away from our herd of seamares once we get them back. I don't care how you do it, but keep her away."

Thakur looked her in the eye and answered, "Yes, clan leader."

It took Thakur most of the rest of the day to find Newt, and when he did, he could see she was angry. But the longer she glared at him, the more her flattened ears began to droop. Savagely she turned her head away then looked at the ground between her paws.

Thakur sat down. She glared at him again, then hissed, lifting her lame foreleg with claws bared. "Paw can scratch," she said. His eyes followed the motion of her foreleg. She was right; she had gained enough flexibility and strength in the limb that she could strike out with that forepaw.

"Thakur go now," said Newt sullenly, lapsing into

her rhyming, "or will say yow." She waved the paw at him, swishing her tail.

"Thakur hurt Newt," she said accusingly.

"Newt hurt Thakur too," he answered, not letting her break his gaze. "You wrecked the pen we built."

"Thakur and . . . others took . . ." Newt faltered, stumbling on her lack of words for what she wanted to say. She tried again. "Big one, little one, they swim." She made an odd paddling motion, spreading the toes of her foot to suggest the webbed, splayed feet of the sea-mares.

Thakur felt a sting of guilt, even though he had tried to dissuade Ratha from taking more seamares. "Why didn't you come to me?"

"Me," Newt said echoing him. "Seamares free because of me. Thakur see?"

"I asked you to stay away from that pen. Now I'm in trouble for helping you, and you are in more trouble if any of the Named catch you there again. Why didn't you come to me instead?"

She jerked her head up and stared at him with a strange new bitterness. "Come to you. Come to Dreambiter as well. She walks with you. Her smell. Her track. Newt knows."

Thakur felt himself on uncertain ground.

Newt's eyes narrowed. "Thakur knows too. And doesn't speak."

"I haven't said anything because I don't know enough yet about what happened to you. And if you think you have the right to attack one of the Named because you smell her in your dreams, I'm sorry, but I won't let you do that."

"Named." Newt wrinkled her nose. "Named, lamed."

Her derisiveness and her accusations were starting to get under his skin. "You're only describing yourself, Thistle-chaser," he retorted, letting his temper get the better of him. Then he froze and snapped his jaw shut, but it was too late. She had heard that last utterance.

"Thistle-chaser?" Newt said the word slowly, as if tasting it. Thakur could see feelings fleeting through her eyes like clouds being whipped across the sky by a harsh wind. For an instant her eyes were brighter and clearer than he had ever seen them, then a shroud of pain wiped away the brightness.

He swore inwardly at himself. The last thing he had intended to do was use the name as a weapon, but she had goaded him into flinging it at her. And why had he used it? Because he knew from the feeling in his belly that this was Ratha's daughter.

Newt stayed still, turned far inward. Slowly her legs gave way beneath her, and she sagged until her chin lay on the ground. Her chin moved slightly as she muttered the name again.

Thakur began to think she had gone into a gentler form of her usual fit, when she suddenly bounced up and limped around him in circles, whimpering and rubbing her nose with a forepaw.

"Newt, what's wrong?"

"Thistle. Hurts. Jumped on. Hurts."

He caught her long enough to pry her paw away from her nose and look to see if there was a thorn embedded but found nothing. Her circling became more frenzied and then degenerated into a series of short jumps back and forth, as if she was dodging something only she could see.

"Go to him. He will help. Not to the Dreambiter. Says she'll never learn . . . eyes are empty," she babbled. Now she was bounding around on her three legs like a cub at play, but at every other step a shudder went through her as if she had collided with something unseen. Thakur felt chilled. This was unlike any of her other fits, and it seemed to have complete possession of her. Afraid she was gone for good, he caught up with her and laid a paw on her, trying to halt her mad dance.

"Thistle. Hurts. Go to him. No, Dreambiter!" Newt cried, her voice rising. She leaped in the air, writhing, twisting, slashing out with claws and teeth at the ghost in her memory. One wild swipe caught Thakur on the side of the jaw. He pounced on her, trying to hold her down until the fit loosed its grip, but she wiggled free and shot off down the path toward the cliff edge. To his horror she did not slow or turn aside but ran right over. He heard a faint scrabbling, a yowl, several soft bumps, and then a terrifying silence.

Legs and tail trembling, Thakur forced himself to walk to the edge and peer over. He was afraid he would see nothing except the sea washing back and forth over the rocks, or perhaps a limp form, broken by the fall. When he looked down, he saw at once that the cliff was not as high or sheer as he had feared. It fell away in a series of ledges. On the lowest one, he caught sight of Newt, lying with one paw dangling and her head turned to one side. A tail length below her, the waves surged against the sandstone shelf.

Anger and guilt clawed at him. This wasn't his fault, he growled to himself. Newt had provoked him into using the name he had learned from Ratha. She had run down the path and blindly over the edge. If anything had killed her, it was her craziness and unpredictability. Thakur argued with himself, but he could not turn away. Something held him frozen at the clifftop, staring down at Newt.

She lay still, but she was breathing. He could see there was no blood. Nor were there contorted limbs or other indications of serious injury. It was likely that she had slid down the steep slope, bounced over the upper ledges, and knocked herself out before coming to rest at the bottom.

Quickly Thakur began searching for a safe path down to the ledge where she lay.

A network of narrow shelves and ledges wove down the sloping face. Thakur found that he could keep his balance by leaning against the rock wall and placing one foot directly ahead of the next. He kept his eyes on the path, not letting them stray to the surf crashing below. Slowly he crept down each downsloping ledge until it intersected the next or gave out. Those were the worst moments—when he had to back himself over the edge, hind feet searching for the shelf below while he hung by his foreclaws. On one such drop he nearly unbalanced and toppled over but managed to catch himself.

Slowly he worked his way back and forth across the cliff face until he was a few tail lengths above Newt. He saw her stir, draw the dangling paw up, turn her head, swallow. He went a few more steps along the narrowing ledge then saw something else. The seawater beneath

Newt's ledge churned, and then the shape of a seamare loomed underneath. The creature lifted its head above the waves and pointed its muzzle at the shelf where Newt lay. Another shape surfaced beside the first—smaller, more agile.

Thakur halted and watched the seamare and seacolt. Were these the two Newt had befriended? Now both muzzles pointed upward at the rock, as if the pair could sense Newt was there and needed help. Splayfoot reached up with her black paws, but she could only scrabble uselessly at the sandstone base. A wave lifted Guzzler, and he tried to reach the ledge, but the retreating swells dropped him back before he managed a hold.

Thakur lowered his head and crept on down the path. The seamares couldn't get to Newt. She would need his help. Two startled bellows from below made him stare at the beasts, who glared back at him and showed their tusks. He wondered how long he would last if he fell into the water with them.

He went another few steps. Splayfoot started to roar, throwing herself as high against the cliff as she could. Though unnerved by the noise and by the seamare's frenzied efforts, Thakur did everything he could not to threaten her. He kept his teeth covered and his ears forward. He talked to her in the same tone he used when dealing with restive herdbeasts.

"Easy, easy. I'm Newt's friend, just as you are, you duck-footed dappleback. You just stay down there and keep quiet."

An indignant roar nearly blew him off the shelf as soon as he laid a paw on Newt. Again he fought to keep his balance and not to look down into the long, cavernous vault of the seamare's open jaws. He ignored her long enough to give Newt a quick going-over. She had a few bruises and a lump on her head but nothing worse. He looked back the way he had come. Could he take her back up that steep path? He had barely made it down himself, and she was both shaky and lame. No. He knew if he tried, they would both fall.

Splayfoot roared at him again, accompanied by honks from Guzzler.

"You know, both you and I are after the same thing," Thakur said reasonably. "We've got to get Newt off this cliff. Perhaps we can come to an understanding of sorts."

The seamare clamped her jaws shut, eyeing Thakur as she bobbed in the water. It became clearer and clearer to him that the only way to get Newt off the ledge was by sea. And he'd have to do it soon. He could see that the tide was retreating, pulling the water level down and increasing the drop from the ledge into the breakers below.

A rumble came from the seamare, warning him of another indignant blast, but at the last minute Splayfoot seemed to change her mind. With a snort that blew spray from her nostrils, the seamare reared up. He could see her snuffle the wind that blew across his coat, and he was suddenly thankful he still bore the pungent stink of seamare dung.

Splayfoot bobbed in the surf, turning her head from side to side as if she didn't know what to make of this strange intruder.

Thakur tried to wake Newt. She responded, but she was still groggy. Gently he turned her head so she looked down into the ocean.

"There are your friends," Thakur said softly. "They will help you."

"Newt go," she whimpered, peering over the edge. Splayfoot heaved herself up again, lifted by a wave, but this time she didn't roar, only stretched her neck to touch noses with Newt. Thakur watched as Newt tried to climb down. She was too shaky and frightened to do much more than lean down off the shelf.

"Here. Turn around. Lower yourself feet first, like I did," he said, nudging her. Taking her scruff in his jaws as she backed over, he dug in his rear claws to hold himself and braced his forepaws to keep from sliding. Carefully he lowered her, stretching until his neck ached so that she would have as short a drop as possible.

Just before he let her go, he lost his clawhold. Reflexively his jaws opened, but he couldn't save himself and fell into the surf between the two seamares. The surging water caught him, tumbled him over and around until he no longer could find the surface and thought he would drown. A blunt nose underneath the belly pushed him roughly, and somehow his head rose above the water. He gasped. Then a broad back rose beneath him until he lay on top of it, his paws clasping the sides of the big sea-beast.

Splayfoot rolled her eyes and gave a disapproving grunt, as if she wasn't sure she should be helping him. Nearby Newt paddled weakly, buoyed up by Guzzler. She still looked dazed, but she had recovered enough to recognize Thakur. Slowly the odd party swam away from the cliff base, around a small point, and landed at Splayfoot's cove near the jetty.

Shivering, Thakur waded to shore. Newt hobbled up

the beach, shaking herself as she went. She disappeared between two rocks, and Thakur guessed she was heading for her hideaway.

He turned to look at the two seamares, who were lying half-submerged in the lapping waves, staring back at him.

"I don't know if you did that for Newt's sake or mine," he said aloud, watching their ears swivel, "but I'm grateful." He thought then about leaving Newt to herself, for he was wet and tired, but he knew he should go after her.

He was halfway up the beach before he realized that Newt's fear and headlong flight had proved something he could not have learned in any other way. There was no doubt now. Though he swore he would never say that name to her again, he knew Newt was Ratha's daughter, Thistle-chaser.

Newt huddled against the sandstone wall of her cave, trying to isolate herself from the one who had crept in after her. Part of her knew it was Thakur, but the frenzied, frightened part of her knew him only as a shadow who walked with the Dreambiter. He had tried to curl up next to her and speak to her, but his words were only a dim buzzing in her ears, and his presence drove the cold fear deeper. She struck out at him, clawing and biting, trying to drive him out. But though he withdrew, he stayed close, and she could only huddle by herself.

She remembered when she had been able to see Thakur as warm and real, not just as a shade allied with the enemy of her dreams. She knew she could lay her head against his flank and gain comfort from him. Sometimes she had been able to let herself slide into the fantasy that he was the kind one with the dark-copper face and amber eyes, who had loved her without judging.

But now all she could see were Thakur's eyes, and they burned green, like the Dreambiter's.

Newt curled up tightly, shuddering. She knew Thakur was there, but she could not let him come near. Not after he had spoken the word that broke through the barriers around her memories. Not after he had let the Dreambiter loose.

Her head throbbed and buzzed. She buried her muzzle between her paws, trying to fend off the rising panic. She could feel the Dreambiter prowling the caves of her mind, pacing deliberately toward the hole Thakur had made with that terrible word . . . that was somehow her name. She trembled, knowing the demon was real and could come down on her at any time, no longer held back or confined by her will.

Newt cried her misery to the cave wall, wishing it could somehow move or answer. The cave only seemed to close in around her, becoming a trap instead of a shelter. If the Dreambiter rose again, where would she flee? Would the terror chase her blindly over a cliff again or just make her run until she died from exhaustion?

A strange calmness settled over her, though she knew it was just a lull. It gave her strength to remember the other times when the Dreambiter had attacked, wounded, and then fled. She knew those skirmishes were over. The Dreambiter had grown strong. Now it would attack to kill.

*　*　*

Thakur crouched at the mouth of Newt's cave, alarm making the fur rise all over his body as he watched her. He desperately wanted to comfort her, but each time he tried to curl up beside her, he had been met with a blind, slashing attack that drove him away. And then she writhed and muttered or drew up in a pitiful huddle.

That he could only watch and do nothing made him feel trapped and helpless. The scratches she had given him stung and bled, but because her swipes were wild and uncontrolled they were only annoying. Pity and anger wrenched at him, making him creep closer once again.

Her smell alone made him flatten his ears, for rage and despair poured from her like a thick, choking fluid. But it was her words that held him close, that made him risk another flurry of claws and teeth.

". . . kill you, Dreambiter, find you kill you . . . smell is real, you are real, no more hurting ever ever ever . . ."

"Newt!" Thakur hissed, but she only jerked and started to writhe in a way that made him wonder if she was dying.

He felt cold and exhausted. Closing his eyes, he confessed to himself that he did not have the strength to endure any more or the skill to soothe her pain. He had to have help. He could feel himself shaking and knew he would be useless both to himself and Newt if he kept struggling. Perhaps one of the females: Bira could be gentle and comforting.

He grimaced in irony. No. The one who really held the key was the Dreambiter herself: Ratha. He had allowed her to evade responsibility for what she had done to her daughter. Not just Ratha alone, but perhaps all of the Named together could do something to help. And if Thistle-chaser was dying, Ratha should know.

"Newt," he hissed softly. "I can't do this alone. I need help. Stay here. I won't be gone long."

Thakur turned away from the cave, but he could not help hearing the tortured voice saying over and over again that the price of this pain would be the Dreambiter's life.

CHAPTER 12

RATHA PACED toward Fessran's new lair, hating the tightness that grew between her shoulders with every step she took. Fear stole the fluidity from her stride, the suppleness from her muscles, until she felt wooden.

She wished that Fessran had taken Mishanti and gone beyond her reach. But no. Instead, the Firekeeper had chosen to den nearby and, even worse, to walk on Named ground, leaving footprints whose mixed odors said that the Firekeeper had fostered the witless cub and openly defied the orders of the clan leader.

Sand and salt grass lay under Ratha's feet now, but the path she trod was the same in bitterness as the trail she had taken before to Fessran's den when the Named had lived on clan ground.

Last time, Thakur had made the journey with her.

This time she would make it alone. There was only one cub to carry from the lair, but that would not lessen the difficulty of the task. The ache in her jaw from the litterling's weight would be the least of the pains she would know.

And Fessran had already named the cub and kept the name, in defiance of Ratha's order: Mishanti. The word beat in Ratha's mind, whispered like the salt grass tearing past her legs. A name worthy of a cub who could bear it and know what it meant to be set apart by the gift of a word—a name—that carried the essence of selfhood. Ratha drew back her lip in scorn at Fessran's foolishness. A name was worse than useless to a cub who could not use it.

She clung to one hope: that the remaining rags of the friendship she and Fessran had known might make Fessran surrender the cub without a fight. That hope dwindled when she topped a rise that led to the den and looked down to see a sand-colored form pacing the ground. A fire burned beside the lair.

Now the tightness crept from between Ratha's shoulders to a place in her chest, between her front legs. Would Fessran use the Red Tongue against her? The Firekeeper looked rough, wild, her belly drawn except for the swollen teats she used to nurse the cub. Her face was taut.

She stopped pacing and stood, her gaze fixed. Ratha slowed but did not stop.

"The trails we take turn back on themselves, clan leader," Fessran hissed, reminding Ratha that she too remembered how they had stood facing each other when Ratha had come to take Shongshar's cubs. That time,

Fessran had seen the truth and backed down. Perhaps now . . .

"No, Ratha." The Firekeeper's voice was low and shaking. "I wasn't sure then. I know now. You are wrong about Mishanti. The light in his eyes is hard to see, but it is there."

"Has he spoken? Has he done anything to show he has the gift we seek?"

"Not yet. But that doesn't matter. Not to me."

Ratha ground her back teeth in frustration over Fessran's willing blindness. She knew the depth of loss and loneliness that could twist things and make an impossibility into a forlorn hope.

"Let me see him again," she said wearily. Fessran went into the den and brought Mishanti out. She lay beside him, guarding him with a forepaw, gazing down at him and licking the top of his head.

"I don't know why I love him," she said softly, "but I do." She gathered him in with both forepaws. He fell against her breast, snuggled up against her with his paws waving. "Why do we love cubs?" she asked Ratha, looking up with eyes that were angry and pleading. "Why, when they cause so much fuss and trouble, when they grow up and forget who you are, or when they die and you have nothing left?"

Ratha found herself unable to answer. At last she said, "Fessran, this season has been difficult for all of us. And I didn't realize . . ."

"Do you know why I'm so sure about him, Ratha?" Fessran interrupted suddenly. "Because at night, when I'm lying in the den with him, smelling his scent, I can see what he will be. In the dark I can see him running along a hill crest with a torch in his mouth, his fur silver and his eyes flame. And that fire will burn for the Named, if you give it a chance."

Ratha stared at Fessran, not knowing what to say. She wondered if the strain of the drought and the move had somehow pushed Fessran onto trails that led beyond reality.

She tried to steer Fessran away from her vision and her strange conviction. Softening her voice, she said, "I know you can't help loving cubs. It's part of what you are. Most of the clan sees the Fessran who is the Firekeeper leader, who calls others soft as dung about treelings, who chews the ears of anyone who gives her any nonsense. I have seen the one who ran beside me with the Red Tongue, and I also see the one who loves cubs. But this cub is a mistake. He won't be able to give back what you are giving him. Please understand. I'm not trying to be cruel either to you or to him."

Fessran's gaze pierced her. "Do you really know by looking at a cub's eyes what he will be like? Do you have some infallible gift that says this one can be Named and this one cannot? I don't think so. It isn't as easy as that. And I don't think you are as sure as you pretend to be."

"I'm not," Ratha admitted. "But what my eyes and my nose and my belly tell me is that this cub is worthless to the clan. Khushi never should have brought him, and you never should have kept him."

"Is that how you think of him?" Fessran's gaze and voice had a raw edge. "As something that just happened? A creature that died and must now be buried?"

"An Un-Named one whose grandsire probably left

those scars in your shoulder," Ratha said, hardening her voice.

Fessran flattened her ears. "You think you'll frighten me with that again? Oh no. Just because Shongshar's blood may run in this cub is no reason to say he will have to grow up that way. It was not just Shongshar's long teeth that led him to take the trail he did."

Ratha broke off and stared at the cub, trying to find some indication that she was wrong after all. But Mishanti was diffident, refusing to answer her gaze and turning his head away in the shy way of the Un-Named. What Ratha could see of his eyes held little promise. She swallowed hard, wishing for Fessran's sake that there was *something*. But she couldn't lie to herself or to Fessran.

"I cannot accept him in the clan, Firekeeper."

The dregs of Fessran's hope seemed to run out of her, making her shrink down. To Ratha's eyes she seemed to grow thinner, harder. Only her eyes held a trace of softness, and that was for the cub she guarded. Mishanti arched his back, rubbing his little spike of a tail under her chin.

Ratha saw doubt flicker at the edge of her eyes like a snake's tongue and seized it.

"Fessran, this is a blind trail you run, an empty husk, a dried bone. Next birthing season, you will have your own cubs. Save your love for them." Ratha paused. "I promise I will not kill this cub. I will take him to the same place as I took the others. At least one of those survived. Perhaps he will too."

"But I will never know him," Fessran said in a dried-up, desperate voice. "Don't you understand that? I will never know him."

"There is nothing there to know," Ratha said in a low voice that started to turn into a growl.

"How can you be so sure?" Fessran cried. "You're not, are you? You are afraid. Afraid of something I don't understand. You are more frightened by this than you were of Shongshar. What is it, then, that stalks you, and makes you turn and strike out, even if the one before you is only a litterling?"

Fessran's words struck deep, as if into the heart of a flame, and the sparks they threw coalesced into Thistle-chaser's face. Ratha shuddered, squeezed her eyes shut, and thrust the memory aside. No, she could not face that, not even now.

"All right. I'll tell you what I fear. You know that there is something in our kind that sets us apart from the others around us. There are very few of us and many of the Un-Named. Why we have come to be, I don't know. Why we have the gift that lights our eyes, I don't know either."

"We are more clever than the Un-Named," Fessran grumbled. "Is that such a big difference?"

"No, it is not just cleverness. It is something else that we don't have a word for. It is what makes us Named and the others not." Ratha drew a breath. "And what frightens me is I know we can lose this gift. When I was exiled from the clan after I brought the Red Tongue before Meoran, I walked trails with the Un-Named. Some were as clever as we, others no better than herdbeasts, but many stood somewhere between. It was they who frightened me most of all, for what I saw in their eyes was that gift fading away. . . ."

But it was what I saw in Thistle-chaser's that tore me most of all.

Fessran looked away. "So those who do not have this gift taint us if they come near?" She snorted. "Sometimes I wonder if we aren't the ones who are tainted. What has this gift you speak of really brought us? The sharper the fang, the deeper wound it can give and the worse pain." She looked down at Mishanti. "The Un-Named do not have to judge their own and cast them aside. And when the judgment comes from fear, clan leader?"

"Then blame me and leave the marks of blame on my coat. But I have to do what is right for our people," Ratha said. "The cub must be taken from clan territory so that he does not mate with females of the Named. And he must go now, so that the pain of his going is less."

Fessran lowered her chin over the cub and raised her hackles. "Mishanti is mine."

"I won't fight you, Fessran," Ratha said quietly. "You may deny the power of Shongshar's teeth, but the wound they gave you will tell."

Pain whipped the Firekeeper's face into a mask of slitted eyes and bared teeth. The eyes were wild with the knowledge that Ratha's words were bitterly true; that if it came to a fight, Fessran would lose.

"Give him to me. Now."

Suddenly the eyes were gone from in front of her, and Fessran became a sand-colored streak that blurred the ground near the fire. The Red Tongue spit sparks as Fessran dug a torch into its heart and lifted the flame aloft. Her jaw trembled so that her teeth shuddered against the torch shaft, but she swung the flame around so that it blocked Ratha from Mishanti.

The shock of seeing the Red Tongue raised against her in Fessran's jaws seemed to wrench the ground from beneath Ratha's feet. She staggered, squeezed her eyes shut. She opened them again to find the one who had been her friend standing before her with a flaming torch.

"Will you burn me with my own creature?" she hissed. "Maybe you would be right to do so. The two gifts of the Named burn too brightly and leave only ashes."

A wordless, agonized howl broke from the Firekeeper. The firebrand swung, but it went past Ratha and soared free back into the fire-nest. Fessran faced Ratha, her sides heaving. "Take him then, because I can't kill you. Because my cursed memory still lets me see the times when you and I ran the trails together, carrying the Red Tongue in our jaws." She took a shuddering breath. "But before you go, you should know something else: You drove your own daughter away for the same reason you are tearing Mishanti from me."

Ratha felt a shock go through her body, almost paralyzing her. "How do you know this? I never told anyone. You're good at lying, Firekeeper. I almost believed you."

"Thakur told me some of the truth, and the rest I found myself," Fessran said. "She has nightmares about you, falls into fits when she catches your smell. She calls you the Dreambiter and would kill you if she could. Newt is yours, Ratha. Half-witted, crippled—she is your daughter."

"No," Ratha growled.

"And I'll tell you something else. I think she's out there, watching, listening to your words."

Again Thistle-chaser's spotted face was before Ratha, distorted, crying out in pain. Then Newt's face overlaid it, but the eyes were still the same. They swirled, taunting her. Could Fessran be right? Was the one who had been Thistle-chaser out there listening?

Ratha shook herself. She could not be distracted. Not now.

She lunged at Fessran, driving her back from the bewildered Mishanti.

"Take him!" the Firekeeper howled. "Take him and then, maybe, I will be able to hate you enough to feed you your own creature and make you live by your own law."

Another cry broke from her, a cry that seemed to tear Ratha from inside. She shook with the pain of it and ached to offer the Firekeeper some scraps of comfort, but all she could do was take the cub by the scruff and go.

Thakur had heard Fessran howl before, but rarely had there been such raw grief and rage in the Firekeeper's voice. The sound drew him to the vale behind Newt's lagoon, and he went quickly, with Aree crouching on his shoulder. As he was starting up the path, Fessran appeared, galloping past an outcropping. She nearly ran into him.

He dodged to the side while she skidded, raising a plume of fine dust and sand that set her coughing. Her ribs lifted in sobbing breaths.

"Did you see Ratha?" she managed to ask.

"No. What happened?"

"She came and took Mishanti. The cub I kept and wanted to adopt."

"That's what set you off running and yowling? Fessran, I can't stop Ratha from doing what she thinks is best for the clan," he argued.

"Then why are you here?"

"I need help. Something's happened to Newt. She went wild, ran off a cliff. She wasn't killed, but she went into one of her fits, and she can't or won't come out of it."

Fessran stared at him. "What, by the Red Tongue's ashes, did you do to set that off?"

"I lost my temper and I called Newt by her name. Her real name. Thistle-chaser. I think hearing it brought back all sorts of things."

"So that proves it. She is Ratha's daughter. I told Ratha that. I told her she had no right to take Mishanti, but I couldn't stop her. If we both go after her?"

"I can't leave Newt. Something's really gone wrong with her. Please, Fessran," he pleaded as he saw the Firekeeper stare angrily down the trail in the direction that Ratha had probably gone. "Come with me. At least help me find Bira or someone."

"If I help, will you come with me to talk some sense into Ratha?"

Wearily Thakur agreed, then led the way back to the cave where he'd left Newt. Apprehensively he approached, listening for muttering or other sounds. He heard only silence and his own footsteps. Crouching down, he peered into the cave, feeling a lump come into his throat when he found everything quiet and still. But when his eyes grew used to the darkness, he saw Newt had gone.

For an instant he stayed there, feeling numb and puzzled. Where could she have gone? Why would she have left? And then the answer came, for he remembered her last words as he'd left the cave: She had gone to hunt the Dreambiter.

He scrambled out, ruffling his fur backward in his haste. Nearby he saw Fessran nosing a set of pawprints in the wet sand.

"These certainly aren't yours," the Firekeeper said. "Well, Newt can't be dying if she's up and wandering around." She stared at Thakur. "What's the matter now?"

He tried to halt the fear racing through him. "Fessran, she was raving about killing the Dreambiter. I think she's gone after Ratha."

"Newt?" Fessran howled derisively, but her voice shook. "She couldn't take a newborn herdbeast! If she tries to fight Ratha, she'll get ripped in so many pieces we'll never find them all."

Thakur heard her fall silent under his stare. She looked away from him, then back again.

"Don't tell me you think that lame little half-wit could . . ."

"Newt is not a half-wit, Fessran. Far from it." Thakur kept his voice and his gaze even. "I warned Ratha not to underestimate her, and she didn't listen. It may cost the Named dearly."

The Firekeeper raked the ground, glared at Thakur. "I want Mishanti back. I want Ratha to see she is wrong. But I don't want her to have to die for it!"

"Then you and I will have to find her before Newt does," Thakur said, his voice icy.

"Can Newt really . . ." Fessran faltered.

"She can," Thakur answered grimly. "I'm the one to blame for that. I helped her heal her leg." He remembered how wildly Newt had fought when in the grip of her fit, how he had to hold her down with all his strength. And he knew how brightly her rage burned against the Dream-biter.

"All right. I'm coming," said Fessran. "For Mishanti's sake, if not Ratha's."

"And for your own, though you'd never admit it," Thakur snapped back. "Hurry!"

He heard Fessran's feet behind him as they galloped off together down the path. Thakur had a good idea of where Ratha might be headed. If she'd taken Mishanti, she probably intended to make the journey to the same place where she'd abandoned Shongshar's cubs several seasons ago. She would have to use the same trail back up to the coast range that he had used on his first journey to the beach. The way was a little different now. Instead of having to ford the inlet of the estuary that lay across the trail, she would cross on the floating bridge moored to the bank. It occurred to Thakur that such a crossing would be a good place for an ambush.

He begged more speed from his paws as he headed toward the raft-bridge, planning to catch Ratha there or at least find her footprints. It wouldn't be easy. Newt had a head start. He could only hope that her healing foreleg would not stand the strain and that she would falter despite her revenge-madness. But he knew hoping wasn't enough to save Ratha. He ran faster.

CHAPTER **13**

AS RATHA PADDED through the salt grass with Mishanti in her jaws, she eyed the floating bridge with mixed feelings. She was glad she would not have to make the trip around the inlet. Her jaws already ached from carrying the cub by the scruff, and her conscience hurt her almost as badly. The bridge would save her some travel, but she didn't like the way it shifted and strained against the cords that anchored it to stumps on the bank. Currents riffled water against the upstream side as the retreating tide drew water from the inlet.

The Named had crossed the floating bridge enough times to prove its worthiness. It was her own bad luck that she had to cross on an outgoing tide, but the bridge would bear her.

Lifting her chin to hold Mishanti high, she took several steps down the bank. Was that a splash in the water upstream, she wondered, and what was that eddy? She cocked her head to one side so she could see past the cub in her jaws. A shadow seemed to cross the bottom, but it went swiftly and was chopped up by the small white-caps. She stared hard but could see nothing.

Clouds scudded by overhead, casting fleeting shadows along the ground and over the water. The cub sagged in

Ratha's jaws. With a toss of her head, she heaved him up again and strode onto the floating bridge.

With the first step, the raft-bridge rocked, as she had expected it to. The next few steps were staggers; the mass of bound driftwood and rushes heaved as if it had been struck from beneath. Ratha nearly lost her hold on the cub in her mad scramble to keep on her feet on the plunging raft. But she lost her balance, flopping on her side and clawing wildly to keep atop the mass of thatch and sticks. Mishanti squealed in pain from the pressure of her teeth in his scruff, and her neck muscles strained with the effort of keeping him from tumbling off.

Angrily she vowed never again to use this flimsy crossing during an outgoing tide. Her anger turned to alarm as she felt one end of the raft-bridge swing downstream. She snapped her head around, causing a squall from her small charge. Surely the other tether would hold. But she saw to her horror that the cord lay loose on the surface of the water. The raft surged beneath her and floated away free, carrying her with it.

She crouched, digging her claws into the thatch and holding the cub in her mouth. Her muscles tensed for a jump to the bank, but the shore retreated. She faced the green-gray water, ready to plunge in and stroke for shore. But she knew she could not keep her head above water with Mishanti in her jaws. All she could do was cling to the raft as it headed seaward, bucking and bounding as if it were alive and rejoicing in its escape.

Seeing the tether from the front end streaming alongside her, Ratha extended a claw and snagged the twisted bark-cord. It looked stout, but it must have frayed. Then she looked more closely at the soggy end draped across her paw. Yes, the fiber looked worn, but the final cut was clean, as if someone had chewed on the rope to weaken it and then, at the final moment, bitten through.

She guessed that the other tether would look the same. Crouching, she ground her back teeth while her fangs held Mishanti's scruff. He was a mute, wet little ball of fur by now, hanging limp in her jaws, too terrified to struggle or mewl.

The raft gave an odd lurch that wasn't part of the rhythm of the water bearing it. Ratha loosed her mouth-grip on Mishanti, pressing him down with her chest and hoping he would have enough sense to dig in his claws. She risked a glance over her shoulder at the back of the raft.

Two paws stuck up out of the frothing water, with claws driven deep into sodden thatch and driftwood. One paw was smaller than the other, the leg shrunken. Soaked fur revealed the bony outlines of the leg and the corded tendons in each foot.

From the instant she had recognized that the raft's tethers had been bitten through, Ratha had known her opponent was Newt. Now the knowledge hit her again, this time with such bitter force that it threatened to jolt her off the raft. To Newt, she was a nightmare, a tormentor. And Newt was Thistle-chaser, the daughter she had bitten, then deserted. She could no longer deny to herself that this vengeful enemy was her own flesh and Bonechewer's legacy. How could there be anything between them except hate?

Ratha felt ice freeze in her belly. She was no stranger to hate. Many had opposed her and tried to thwart her rise to clan leader or topple her from leadership. She had faced Meoran, the old clan leader, and then Shongshar, but neither could claw as deeply to her heart as this water-soaked, green-eyed revenge that fought to hang on to the raft.

She will give her own life if she thinks she can take mine, Ratha thought, and knowing that sent the ice creeping out along her limbs. *Thakur and Fessran, why did you meddle? You did her no favor by finding a mother who should have stayed lost.*

The raft slid with the tidewater toward the sea. Ratha stared numbly at the white surf line ahead and flattened her ears against the increasing rumble and crash of the waves. A roller crested ahead of the raft then broke, drenching her. The sea's churning whitecaps took the raft and spun it around so rapidly that Ratha closed her eyes from dizziness. One whirl took the craft so close to shore that she tensed to jump, but before she could get her feet beneath her, a strong seaward current swept the raft away again.

Though Newt might be smaller and lame, she had maneuvered Ratha into alien and treacherous surroundings, where she held the advantage. Ratha, the proud bearer of fire on land, was but a ragged wretch clinging to a few sticks in the sea.

The current weakened, giving the raft less forward motion, but the chop and roll tossed it about more than ever. Ratha clung to the slithering mass of thatch and driftwood. Drenched and cold to the point of numbness, she nestled Mishanti between her forelegs, holding his nape in her jaws and trying to shield him from the spray. Even now she was wondering if she could manage to swim ashore without drowning him.

The fierceness of the attack told Ratha that Newt was ruthless and remorseless enough to kill her. Was her daughter mad, like one taken with the foaming sickness? No, Newt's illness was not the foaming sickness, for that killed rapidly. It was something slower, more subtle, and even more destructive. Newt's attack was more than purposeless madness. It had been planned with a cold cunning that had outdone the best of the Named.

Knowing that there was a deep and painful reason for Newt's hatred drew Ratha's strength from her. She closed her eyes again, not from dizziness but from despair. *I sought the light in Thistle-chaser's eyes. I have found it now, but it is a light that sears me more than the touch of the Red Tongue.*

Her fear hardened despair into harsh resolution. This ex-cub might have good reason to vent revenge on her. That didn't matter anymore. If Newt attacked, she must fight back, not only for her sake but for the sake of the Named, who would be left without a leader. Perhaps, she thought, she might be able to somehow talk to Newt, and if the chance came, she would take it. But if it came down to teeth and claws, the fact that Newt was Thistle-chaser, her own daughter, would no longer matter.

It was that decision that made her sidle backward, trying to gauge whether she could lash out with her rear claws and break Newt's grip on the raft. If she could do it without wounding her, then Newt could swim to shore. That might make managing the runaway raft and Fessran's adopted cub a little easier.

Ratha's impulse was to strike quickly and get Newt off the raft. Her hind paws trembled but didn't move. She was certain that Newt meant to seek her life, yet something in Ratha still held to the hope that it was only a threat.

She couldn't attack. Not without knowing.

She secured Mishanti once again and craned her head back over her shoulder. The raft had slowed now. Newt was still in the water, hanging on with her claws, but the surging current no longer buried her. As Ratha peered back at her, Newt lifted her chin above the water, her ears flat, her gaze the color of serpentine.

She may understand words. I have to try.

"Thistle-chaser," Ratha said. The ears twitched and flattened more against the brine-slicked head. The chill in the eyes went beyond the cold of the sea. They looked like marble or green-frosted ice.

"Dreambiter," Newt answered, never taking her gaze from Ratha's. Ratha could not control her flinch.

"We can tear each other apart well enough with words. Let it stop there."

"You tear me with teeth, Dreambiter. I answer."

"Leave the raft and swim to shore. I promise none of the Named will hunt you or seek you out," Ratha said.

Newt slitted her eyes. "I hunt you, cub-slayer."

"You have given me to this angry water. I will never reach shore. Isn't that enough? Or will you force me to stain myself with your blood . . . ?"

"Again," Newt hissed, ending the sentence with the word Ratha could not say.

Newt loosed her grip and slid back into the sea. For one hopeful instant Ratha thought she had persuaded her to go. Then she saw a shape glide alongside the raft. Newt lifted her head, bared her teeth, then ducked under. Again Ratha hoped she had gone. She felt the raft lurch once more and sag beneath her. Newt surfaced, her jaws tangled in bark-cord lashing from the bottom of the raft. Ratha watched, feeling numb. Newt was tearing her floating refuge apart.

With slow, deliberate malice, Newt continued to destroy the raft-bridge. She slashed reed bundles, chewed off bindings, and pried driftwood sticks apart. Now Ratha fought back, striking out with bared claws from the narrow and increasingly cramped area that remained to her. But Newt could easily duck into the sea to escape and rise on the raft's far side to plague her again.

Ratha knew that Newt could mount a sharp, quick attack, tearing her throat or pulling her into the sea and dragging her under. Newt wanted more than just her death: She had discovered the savage pleasure of tormenting an enemy.

The sea behind the raft was soon littered with shreds of driftwood, rushes, and bark-cord. Gray water welled up through the floor, soaking Ratha's feet and half covering Mishanti. She tried to hold the fraying mass together with her claws, but Newt relentlessly pulled away one piece after another.

Ratha found herself clinging to the last fragment of the raft, holding the cub in her mouth and staring at the foam-streaked back of a wave. As the swell lifted her, she caught sight of white surf in the distance. Waves breaking meant land of some sort, even if it was no more than a few rocks. She held to the raft as long as she could, then launched herself over Newt's head into the sea.

The shock of cold water punched the breath from her. The weight of the struggling cub dragged at her jaws as she fought to get her nose above water. For one panicky instant, she almost let him go in order to get a precious breath.

She suddenly wondered why she was fighting so hard to save the youngster. Hadn't she taken him from Fessran's den to exile him from the clan? *To abandon him, not kill him*, a hurt part of her cried. The irony of that claim made Ratha cringe with shame as she shivered and struggled in the ocean. Had she really fooled herself into thinking that young cubs taken from their mothers and abandoned far beyond clan ground would survive? *Quit fooling yourself. You were going to kill him. And now you probably will whether you intend to or not.*

With an angry sideways toss of her head, Ratha flung the youngster back over her shoulder, still holding on to his scruff. He slid off, dangling in her jaws and threatening to drown both of them. Once more she tried, giving a fierce kick and a wrench of her neck. He fell across the back of her shoulders and she felt cub-claws drive in deeply, making her snarl with pain.

She wallowed in a trough between waves, searching for some sign of the breakers she had seen from the raft. Disoriented by the swells, she picked one direction and struck out with Mishanti clinging to her neck. A roller lifted her, showing her the distant surf line once again, and she changed her course.

It was slow, hard paddling, with bouts of exhaustion, disorientation, and panic. Several times she lost sight of the breakers and ended up swimming aimlessly. Her breath seared her lungs and the back of her throat. Her limbs felt heavy and the cub on her back even heavier.

And then she saw a shape circling her, and she thought

about all the creatures of the sea, especially those who ate meat. Her heart sank further when she recognized the sleek form gliding around her. The thought came to her that without Mishanti, she would have a better chance against Newt and the ocean.

His eyes are empty. I should let the sea take him.

Ratha growled deep in her throat, angered by the suggestion and at the part of her that made it. She knew that if she sacrificed the youngster, she would be much closer to Newt's image of her. But why did it matter, a part of her cried out, despairing. The cub would die out here anyway.

The stinging pain of claws in her nape told her he wasn't dead yet. She forced herself to stroke with limbs that throbbed with weariness and lungs that burned with ashy dryness, despite all the water around her. And all the time, Newt circled her like a shark, coming in to rake her flank.

Newt's attack was strangely languid, as if she were only sporting. Perhaps she was playing with her quarry as a hunter would toy with prey. Or perhaps she was surprised to see that Ratha had come this far and wondered how much farther she would go before the sea overwhelmed her.

Ratha only fixed her eyes on the tossing surf and struggled toward it.

It seemed to Ratha that she had been swimming forever in a gray, heaving landscape of waves, foam, and sky. Her limbs slowed of their own accord, and she hung in the water, utterly bewildered as to where she was or how she had gotten out here. She was tempted to just lie in the trough between swells and let the waves roll her around until she sank.

Then she felt the soggy weight of the cub on her neck, remembered, and paddled onward. The sting from his claws faded. Either she was growing too numb to feel anything, or he was weakening. That thought stabbed her with alarm, and she redoubled her efforts.

The sight of Newt cruising around helped to wake her cold-muddled wits with a surge of anger and sent her thrashing through the whitecaps.

She panted and gasped, her throat raw from salt and hard breathing, her chest seared with pain. A spume of spray fountained into the air ahead of her, raining down onto her head. The boom of waves breaking against rocks penetrated her dulled hearing.

A little surge of triumph fought its way through the layers of exhaustion and fear, but before she could really feel it, Mishanti started to slide from her neck, too weak to keep his claws fastened in her nape any longer. Again she grabbed him, slung him back into place, hoping the jolt would revive him long enough for her feet to find some purchase on the rocky bottom.

But the rocks where the waves broke seemed to plunge right down into deep water, with no way to scale their sheer faces. With leaden paws and a growing fear weighting her down, Ratha swam behind the surf line, searching for some shoal or shallows where she could drag her weary self ashore.

At last she came to a place where sea-battered stones had split and tumbled, forming a field of islets. Here she might have a chance of getting through before the breakers dashed her against the rocks. She splashed and scrabbled, tearing her pads on mussel shells that encrusted the islets. She floundered on her belly, nearly lost the cub again. Dragging him by his scruff, for she was too weary to lift her head, she clambered up through tidepools, slipping and falling on slick strands of seaweed, while backwash from the surf dragged at her legs.

Her vision, already blurred from exhaustion, threatened to fade completely. Desperately she sought a shelf or slab of rock far enough above the spray to offer some refuge. Just when she thought she would have to collapse atop the jagged crest of the wave-beaten rock, she caught sight of a low, sloping band of sandstone. It was steep and tilted down toward the surf, but it was better than lying on sharp-edged coral and shells. She struggled across the mussel beds, her pads bleeding and throbbing.

At last she found herself crouching on a tiny, worn table of rock that barely rose above the sea. At least her refuge was flat enough so that she wouldn't slip off, but it offered no protection against wind or wave. With no room to stretch out on her side, she huddled up with Mishanti against her chest and fell into an uneasy drowse.

The flapping of wet fur woke Ratha from a sleep that had been too short and often interrupted by spray blown in her face by the wind. Groggily coming awake, she had to blink and stare before her eyes would focus. She felt her skin prickle, but her fur was too wet to bristle and her limbs too weary to respond, even to a surge of anger. Ratha could only watch Newt clamber onto a boulder that stood next to her own refuge.

Newt stopped to shake more brine out of her coat.

Ratha endured a long silence with only the sound of the sea and her daughter's harsh breathing. The gray-green eyes stared at her, never wavering. Their color shifted like the hues on an incoming breaker.

Then Newt came slowly down off her rock and onto Ratha's. Though Ratha's limbs screamed in protest, she gathered up the cub and scuttled away as far as she could go. Head low, eyes fixed, Newt limped after her.

Ratha let Mishanti down long enough to speak. "I can't fight you with him in my jaws."

Newt ignored her words. When Ratha held her ground with the cub between her forelegs, Newt stalked up and stood facing her. Uncertainly, Ratha watched as Newt balanced on her good foreleg, her other one drawn up against her chest. She readied herself to fend off a biting attack, thinking the cripple could not attack with her foreclaws.

Newt's raised paw shot out. A claw dug into Ratha's cheek fur, dragged across her face. Angrily she lashed out with both forepaws, but Newt was too quick. The two faced each other, tails flicking with rage. Quickly Ratha grabbed Mishanti and shoved him to one side. Newt took advantage of the distraction to attack. Again the two met in a brief flurry, scattering fur and droplets of blood before breaking apart.

"Can use this paw now," Newt snarled.

"Thakur told me that he worked with you . . . healed you . . . ," Ratha panted.

"He understood, Dreambiter. He knew."

"But he did stop. After you wrecked the pen . . ."

"Too late. This leg better. Soon Newt will run on all legs, Dreambiter."

Again she launched herself at Ratha, striking in whirl-
wind slashes of claws and teeth. Enraged, Ratha fought
back. She hated the instinct that made her want to seize
Newt's throat and twist until her enemy's neck broke,
yet she knew that was the instinct that would save her
own life. The battle raging inside her was more savage
than the frenzied bursts of combat as the two fought back
and forth across the islet.

"Dreambiter," Newt hissed, closing her teeth around
the word as she stalked Ratha. "Soon I will be free of
you."

Ratha jumped sideways, letting Newt slice empty air.
She hadn't missed by much, and Ratha knew exhaustion
was slowing her. "Your nightmares," she panted.

"No, yours. You run in them. You tear me. Not once,
but again and again and each time the pain comes."

"You think you'll end the nightmares by killing me?"
Ratha spat back. "This thing that strikes at you out of
your dreams is not me. It is something you have made.
Killing me won't put an end to it." Her words were lost
in the rising yowl of Newt's battle cry and the wailing
of the sea wind.

The wind's moan grew shriller, and the waves rolled
higher around the islet, warning Ratha that a squall was
nearing. To spring and dodge as she did on land earned
her only hard, bruising falls on spray-slicked rocks, with
Newt gouging at her belly.

A big wave broke across the islet, drenching them both
and slithering away in a foaming cascade of gray-green
water. A trembling cry struck through the tumult of the
noise and fighting. Ratha saw Mishanti, engulfed by the
retreating water, being dragged away. She leaped, landed

badly on the craggy rocks. One forepaw slipped into a crevice, throwing her hard on her shoulder.

Ignoring the bruising, she tried to pull free but found her foot wedged into the crack. Irritated, she wiggled and jerked fruitlessly. She was stuck, her paw jammed and the cub sliding away beyond her reach.

She lunged, straining the caught leg with her frantic swipes to reach Mishanti with her free paw. As a last, wild effort, she threw herself over, stretching and scrabbling with her rear paws to catch the cub. Her trapped foreleg twisted, sending shooting pain into her breast. For a terrible moment she felt only water against her hind toes, then a wet, sliding body. She caught the cub between her two rear pads and tried to claw him up to where she could grab him. His teeth fastened in her hock in angry protest. Then she could only hang onto him while another wave spilled across the islet.

Even before the water rushed away, she felt him hitching himself up her leg as she lay on the rocks. She looked down and saw his eyes open and burning like amber flames while his needlesharp talons dug into her leg. Something had jolted him out of his numbed terror. Now he was angry, with a fierce rage to live.

Hate me, hate the world, hate everything, but stay alive, Ratha thought at him as he struggled up her wet flank, over her belly, and up her ribs. With a surge of relief, she grabbed him.

A sharp blow bashed her head against jagged rock and nearly stole her consciousness. Against her will, her jaws slackened. The cub slid from her mouth. She cursed herself for having forgotten Newt.

"You can't use your leg, Dreambiter," came the bitter voice. "How does it feel?"

Ratha ignored Newt, lunged groggily to reach the cub, who had tumbled into a tidepool. Her trapped leg sent fiery pains in protest. Again she had almost reached him when Newt caught the flailing paw.

Ratha stared at her daughter as Newt's teeth came down on her leg. Though Newt could not speak now, Ratha read her eyes and seemed to hear words spoken in that flat, cold voice.

You crippled me, Dreambiter. Now you will know how it feels.

"I am not your Dreambiter," Ratha said hoarsely. "I was once, but not now. Listen to me, Thistle-chaser. My death won't kill the creature that torments you. It will make it even stronger."

She curled herself up, kicking out at Newt with rear claws bared, but Newt swung herself aside, yanking Ratha into an even more painful position. Ratha yowled as Newt's teeth sawed against her foreleg. She saw Newt grimace in frustration. A new look, closer to despair than madness, came into Newt's eyes, but the blow to Ratha's head, combined with the grinding pain in her trapped foreleg, had driven her close to oblivion. Newt's face became a blur, along with everything else.

The pain abruptly grew muted. Ratha felt her paw flop free from Newt's jaws. Through the waves of dizziness that washed over her, she heard an angry squall. Struggling to focus her vision, she saw a double image of Newt spinning around to face Mishanti.

"Yow! You bit my tail!" Newt snarled and dealt the

bristling cub a slap that sent him tumbling. Shivering and snarling, he launched himself to the attack once again, leaping between Ratha and Newt. He stood astride Ratha's extended foreleg, his head lowered, short tail lashing. With a growl, he leaped at Newt, making her draw back.

"Get him out of the way," she hissed at Ratha. "Get rid of him, or I'll kill him."

Ratha could only lie still, fighting waves of gray nausea and weariness. Hopelessly she jerked at her trapped foreleg. "Do you think I can?"

Her words only enraged Newt. The sea-green eyes shrank to slits, and the ears flattened against the spray-slicked head. She bared her claws and aimed another blow at Ratha, but again Mishanti flung himself between the two. Ratha struggled to raise her head enough to grab the little warrior in her jaws and yank him aside, but she was too cold and weak. She could only croak out, "No, Thistle-chaser . . ." as Newt struck the youngster.

The cub spun away with two red gashes along his flank, but he rebounded, hurling himself between Ratha and Newt. Again Newt tried to wound Ratha, tore the cub instead. He rolled aside, shuddering, his mouth wide. For one horrible instant, Ratha thought Newt had gutted him; then another gray-green surge of seawater spilled through the rocks. Ratha could feel the wave tug at her, but it wasn't as powerful as the last few.

The cub clung to the jagged rock with his claws as the water streamed around him. It washed the blood away, letting Ratha see the new wound, a long diagonal slash across the lower ribs. When the water retreated, he fought his way back to Ratha, his soaked fur making him look almost skeletal. The welling blood and the too-bright eyes made her feel that he had become something more dangerous than just a litterling.

Again he put himself in front of Ratha, facing Newt. Ratha saw Newt's lips writhe back, baring her teeth. She struggled to make some part of her body move, but she could get only uncoordinated jerks. Newt snapped at the cub, who wobbled aside at the last moment. Again Ratha tried to reach him and failed. Newt was preparing to lunge for the killing bite.

Ratha had only her voice and her wits.

"Dreambiter. Cub-slayer," she snarled, throwing Newt's words back at her.

Slowly Newt's ice-green stare moved from the cub to Ratha. "You are . . ." she began.

"His blood is on your claws now, daughter."

Newt froze, one paw still raised. A tremor crept over her, turning into shivering.

Ratha hitched herself up, trying to hold her daughter's gaze. "You may hate me now, and you may hate me more after I've said this. You will never slay the Dreambiter, because you have become the Dreambiter."

"No."

"You would kill or cripple that cub if it meant you could take out your hate on me. It is the same thing. It was the same thing then."

"No. He in the way," Newt spluttered.

"You got in the way when I attacked Bonechewer," Ratha said, her voice hard. "We are both Dreambiters and cub-maulers. We are both fighting for ourselves so hard that it is easy for us to wound others who get in the way." She paused. "That is the truth, Thistle-chaser."

Now Newt was taking hard, deep breaths. Ratha could see her daughter's rib cage heave. Was it realization or rage that lit the depths of her eyes? Ratha couldn't tell and braced herself for another blow.

With a despairing howl, Newt flung herself around. She seemed to go into a wild fit, slashing at empty air, raking her claws across rocks and opening her jaws in a raw-edged scream. Then she turned her wrath on herself, ripping her own fur with her claws and trying to stab herself with her teeth.

"Thistle-chaser!" Ratha howled, then shut her eyes, unable to bear the sight.

A deep roar drowned out Newt's cries and then there was a booming crash as a storm-lashed breaker surged over the islet. Ratha was caught in a river of icy water that pulled her painfully against her trapped paw. Newt was a mass of soggy fur tumbling between wave crests. And Mishanti was nowhere in sight. Ratha strained as high as she could, trying to spot him. She saw Newt recover, fight her way to a boulder that rose above the water, and cling there, looking dazed.

There was a growing tightness in Ratha's throat. Mishanti, the little warrior who had fought to protect her, had been swept away by the sea. Anxiously she scanned as much of the islet as she could see and then the heaving ocean. Rain began pelting down. Lightning jumped and flickered overhead, and thunder mixed with the roar of beating surf.

And then Ratha saw a tiny, dark shape on the outlying rocks at the far end of the islet. It moved.

"Thistle-chaser!" she called. Newt only stared back at her dumbly.

"The cub—he's down on those rocks. I'm stuck.
Please . . ."

Newt seemed lost in a trance. Ratha turned her gaze
back to the small form nearly lost against the foaming
surf, wondering if he was really still there or whether her
hope had deceived her. A movement at the edge of her
vision startled her. It was Newt, leaving her refuge and
half swimming, half sloshing through the water. She
moved slowly, as if still dazed, but she was going in the
right direction. Toward Mishanti.

She halted, stared at Ratha, her eyes smoky, unreadable.

"Get him," Ratha said. "Not for my sake. For yours."

Newt seemed to wake up. She took several splashing
bounds across the nearly swamped islet, scrambling across
the rocks. She had nearly reached Mishanti when another
wave broke, sending torrents of water over the rocks.
This time the cascade almost drowned Ratha. She fought
to keep her nose above the water, pulling as hard as she
could on her trapped forepaw. Fear stabbed when she saw
foam covering the place where Newt and the cub had
been. Neither one was visible.

Now Ratha was alone. Numbly she hoped the next
wave would engulf her, filling her lungs with water and
giving her a quick choking death. Otherwise she would
hang here on the rocks, battered and soaked, until the
cold killed her. Or grief.

To lose both her daughter and Fessran's foster son to
a single furious sweep of the sea, yet to be left living and
conscious enough to know and feel the loss was cruelty
beyond bearing. Ratha felt herself starting to retreat, to
close down, turning inward to find shelter from the world

around her. Her body was numbed past feeling. She hoped her mind would soon be the same.

A thin wail threaded itself through her dulled hearing. Not until it came again did she even think about lifting her head. It seemed too heavy, not worth the bother. Why the interruption now, when she was starting to feel comfortable? She no longer felt the wind. It was as if she were lying, warm and lazy, in a pool of sun near the entrance to her den.

And then more noises came. Splashes. Panting. Ragged grunts. Ratha forced her eyes open.

Newt struggled in the surf at the islet's edge, holding the cub in her jaws. He looked like a limp fur mat, and when Newt hauled him out, brine streamed from him. Ratha could see that Newt too was nearly at the end of her strength. She shuddered and staggered. Her weak foreleg had taken more of a battering than it could stand and she was limping again.

She had to set the cub down to get her breath. He sprawled on his front, his rapid breathing the only indication to Ratha that he still lived.

"Bring him here," she said to Newt, who gave one final deep breath and took the cub once again in her jaws. She made a quick feint toward Ratha, dropped Mishanti near her, and backed off, as if fearing retaliation. With her free paw, Ratha gathered the bedraggled little bundle to her chest, trying to press some of the seawater out of his coat. She curled around him to warm him with her body and her breath, but she knew she had barely enough warmth to stay alive.

Convulsive shudders went through him, and his eyes began to dull. Ratha knew he was dying of cold. However close she held him, he shuddered harder, and her own clammy coat wasn't helping. She licked the top of his head, full of despair.

Then someone was standing over her. It was Newt. Newt's gaze was uncertain, but there was something new flickering in her eyes that had never been there before.

"My coat thicker," she said. With a clumsiness generated by self-consciousness, she took the shivering youngster from Ratha, shook herself as dry as she could, then curled around him. Ratha watched as Newt ruffed her fur and nestled him into it. After a while he stopped shivering.

"If we can wait out the storm and I can free my paw, we might be able to get to the next islet. I think there is a string of these islets that connects with the jetty where your seamares are." Ratha lifted her head and peered at the sky. Thunder still rumbled overhead, but the rain had lightened to a drizzle, and waves no longer broke so high over their refuge.

She still felt cold outside, but the stabbing despair that was worse than ice around her heart had gone. She dared to hope that they might all get out of this alive and, even more, that things might change between herself and Thistle-chaser.

Waiting for the storm to abate and the seas to calm grew wearying, and Ratha felt the cold creep deeper into her. She had ceased to feel the pain in her trapped paw or the wound on her leg made by Thistle-chaser's teeth. Gradually she slipped into a daze and thought she was again lying in a pool of sun by her den, the sun's rays warm on her coat, sliding through drowsiness into deep sleep.

CHAPTER 14

THISTLE-CHASER LAY near Ratha, trying not to think of anything at all. The events just past were too painful to recall. Bite-and-scratch wounds throbbed and burned all over her body. Some had come from Ratha, others she had inflicted with her own teeth during the fit. She had a scratch on her nose from Mishanti. Though it hurt, she was glad she had saved him, although she still didn't know why. She felt confused, but it was a new kind of confusion: one that promised rather than one that denied.

She wriggled closer to the cub, nestling him in the longer fur covering her belly. Ratha's fur was starting to dry in the fitful wind. Mishanti might be warmer, Thistle-chaser thought, if she sheltered him between herself and Ratha. To get herself and the cub into the right position, she had to lay a paw over Ratha. She didn't want to. It was still frightening to be near this stranger who had somehow given birth to her. She kept her paw in the air above Ratha until it ached with weariness. Gradually she let it sink until her pawpad rested on the fawn-colored fur over Ratha's ribs.

I am touching my Dreambiter, she thought.

To her touch, Ratha felt cold, even colder than Mishanti. She lay stretched out by the pull on her imprisoned forepaw, her head lolled to one side, her mouth half open, her tongue flopping out. It frightened Thistle-chaser.

She is so cold and she doesn't shiver. Dreambiter, wake up. She pawed Ratha gently, then a little more roughly. There was no response.

Dreambiter, why am I afraid you will die? I wanted you to die.

Feeling as though someone else were using her body, she wriggled closer to Ratha, pulling her mother against her chest.

It hurt to hear what you said, but you are right: We are both the same.

Slowly, because she was so frightened, Thistle-chaser spread herself across Ratha as well as Mishanti, trying to warm both of them. She too was shivering, and she wondered if she would die out on this lonely rock. She felt a strange and painful mixture of hope and despair. Perhaps this one who had cast her into such a gray world would be the one to lead her out of it.

But not if you die, Dreambiter. For my sake, please live.

And at last, Thistle-chaser stopped shivering and fell asleep.

Dripping and winded, Thakur scrambled up the crest of an island near the end of the chain that extended from the jetty. Fessran was right behind him, though she faltered, and he had to grab her scruff and haul her up. They had swum and scrabbled from island to island after spotting Ratha adrift on the escaped raft. During one channel crossing, Fessran had encountered a vicious fish with skin that grated like sand and an inclination to take a bite out of anything furry that swam its way.

"I'm sorry," she growled. "You would think that losing my tail tip wouldn't make any difference, but I feel as shaky as a newborn cub." She swung her tail around, licked the torn end. "At least it's stopped bleeding."

"I don't blame you for shaking. I'm a bit unsteady myself. That was just too close."

"Well, I'll remember that cursed fish the next time I'm tempted to dunk myself. It had more teeth than I do. Brrr!"

The two scrambled down over the rocks as seabirds swirled in flocks around them. "This is the last islet, Fessran," Thakur said, not adding that if Ratha and Mishanti weren't on this one, they had been taken by the sea.

They climbed over and around tumbled boulders that had sheared from the cliffs above. Thakur put Fessran in the lead, hoping that would help steady her. He saw her leap atop a flat-topped rock and then freeze where she stood. "They're here," she hissed.

Thakur hopped up beside her and looked out. There, on the last few rocks that met the sea, he saw a rust-and-black pelt sprawled atop a fawn one. His first glance sent a cold wash of dismay through him. Both looked still and stiff enough to be dead. Then he saw the twitch of a rust-and-black tail. Newt still lived. There wasn't enough of Ratha visible to tell.

Beside him, he heard Fessran moan softly and then felt her tense to jump down.

"No, stay here." Thakur put a paw on the Firekeeper's flank.

"Ratha . . . and Mishanti," Fessran choked out.

"I know. But Newt is there too. If she sees you, she may attack us. If I go alone, it will be easier."

"You know my part in this, Thakur," Fessran said in a low voice. "If I hadn't been so angry at Ratha, you might have had a chance to bring the two together."

"We'll talk about that later," Thakur said, his eyes on the two bedraggled forms lying together on the rocks below.

"Mishanti." Fessran tried to keep her voice from shaking. Thakur knew how hard it was for her to wait here, not knowing. Quickly he leaped down off the boulder and scrambled over the rocks. As he approached, he saw Newt stir.

He came alongside her as quietly as he could, then nudged her. Her nose twitched in response to his scent. Her head lifted, wobbly and bleary eyed. As she raised herself, Thakur saw Mishanti curled up between Newt's belly and Ratha's back. His flank rose and fell in a comforting rhythm.

What Thakur could see of Ratha, however, did not look encouraging. Her salt-encrusted fur stood up in spikes, stiffened by bloodstains. Her head lolled to one side, her tongue spilling from slack jaws. Unsteadily Newt half rolled, half crawled to one side, still weak and groggy from exhaustion. "Dreambiter," she hissed softly, stretching out a paw to touch the ragged fawn pelt. "Her foot . . . stuck . . . down between rocks . . ."

Thakur could not see any movement in Ratha's rib cage. His heart sinking, he licked the end of his muzzle and crouched at her head, trying to detect any breath on his dampened nose. He held his own breath until he was nearly dizzy, then let it out in a rush as he felt a tickle of air against his nose-leather.

Quickly he nuzzled Ratha, checking for injuries. He found one forepaw stuck directly down into a crevice, where jagged rock clamped the foot. Gently he nudged her all over, looking for broken bones, but found nothing. She was still breathing, but she was so cold, Thakur thought to himself.

"Tried . . . tried to warm her," Newt said in a thin voice. "She said we both Dreambiters, and she is right, so want her to live."

Thakur began to rub himself against Ratha to warm her and get her alert enough to start moving. He used his tongue on her face and ears, cleaning away salt crystals from the fur around her eyes.

"Come on, yearling," he muttered as he scrubbed. "It would take more than a dunking to kill you. Fessran!" he called over his shoulder to the Firekeeper, who came flying out from behind the rocks. At the sight of Fessran, Newt flattened and retreated.

"She won't hurt you, I promise," said Thakur to Newt. He sent a warning look toward Fessran, but the Firekeeper was taken up with nuzzling Mishanti to make sure he was all right. Then she began licking and rubbing Ratha.

A sneeze was the first indication that Ratha was reviving, then a series of shivers and a moan. Thakur saw her gulp, blink, and open her eyes. Fessran was rubbing her so enthusiastically that the motion pulled Ratha against her trapped foreleg, and she winced with pain.

"Arr! Firekeeper, you always overdo things," she growled. Her gaze turned to Thakur. "I don't know how

you got here, herding teacher, but I'm glad you did."
She tried to lift her head, strained, and sagged back.

Then her gaze traveled to Newt and rested on her
daughter. "I wouldn't have lasted this long if someone
hadn't given me some warmth. I thought you hated me,
Thistle-chaser. Why did you save me?"

Newt hung her head, as if what she had done was
shameful. "I don't know, Dreambiter."

Thakur interrupted. "Don't question her now, Ratha.
Save the questions for later. We have to get you off this
rock." He slid his foreleg under Ratha's chest and tried
to pry upward. Ratha clamped her teeth together and
made no sound, but he could hear her breathing hard in
pain. Her leg was locked fast.

He called Fessran over and both tugged, but with no
greater success. Newt stood to one side, watching, then
started forward to help.

Thakur stopped her. "No good," he said. "All we'll
do is pull her leg off."

He hopped down onto a lower rock, peered sideways
through the crevice where Ratha's paw was stuck. The
cleft widened toward the front, where he was looking in.

"Ratha, if you could pull your leg sideways instead of
straight up, you might have a chance."

She tried, failed. Thakur and Fessran got their jaws
around the upper part of her leg near her chest and tried
to shove her forelimb toward the wider part of the crevice.

They strained and grunted while Newt watched. "No
good," Thakur groaned after several tries. "We'll either
snap our teeth or break her foreleg."

Ratha lay back down. He could see by her panting
and her glazing eyes that she was losing strength rapidly.

"Maybe the leg will have to stay," she whispered softly. "Thistle-chaser has shown me that you can get along without one paw."

Thakur went cold at the idea of having to cripple Ratha to free her. He shot a glance toward Newt. What was she thinking? It would be suitable revenge on Ratha. And Newt's foreleg was much stronger than it had been; she was no longer severely hampered by the old injury. It would be as if the two had changed places.

He studied Ratha's position, how deeply her foreleg extended into the crack and how much room there would be for the horrible task, if they were forced to do it.

"No," he said roughly. "Your leg is in too far. We'd have to work above your elbow, near your chest." He faltered. "You would bleed to death before . . ." He broke off. "There must be another way. There must!"

Jumping down beside the crevice, he peered in once again. If he could somehow snag her stuck foot and yank it sideways, she might be able to get free. He tried to fit his paw in through the opening, but his toes were too large.

"Mishanti," Ratha said, watching him. "A cub's paws are smaller."

"But his leg isn't long enough," Thakur said, still crouched down by the crevice, peering in from the side.

Fessran's yowl interrupted him. "There's a big wave coming. Get up high or hang on!" He saw the Firekeeper grab Mishanti by the scruff. Thakur leaped up beside Ratha, jerked and tugged at her furiously.

"Get the cub and Thistle-chaser to high ground," Ratha growled. "Now!"

With grief tearing at him, Thakur made himself obey,

shepherding a stunned Newt after Fessran, who had already climbed to the highest point on the tiny island. He was still scrabbling for a hold when gray water spilled across the islet. He strained to look back at Ratha. The frothing sea lashed her, robbing her of the last vestiges of warmth she had gained from her daughter and the others. Thakur knew that if they did not get her off the island soon, with or without her foreleg, she would die.

Even before the water drained away, the three were back beside Ratha. Mishanti was left clinging to his perch.

"Newt's got small paws," Fessran said. "And her lame leg is narrower than her good one."

Thakur turned to Newt, but she was already peering into the crack. The thoughts raced in his head. Would she do it? Could she, even if she had the wish to try? Why was she hesitating? Was she judging the situation, or was she just stalling, hoping to force him to cripple Ratha? It would be a suitable revenge, he thought. If she wants it.

Newt lifted her lame foreleg and slowly threaded her paw into the crevice. She gave Thakur an unreadable look. "For my Dreambiter," she hissed.

"For you," he answered softly. Ratha lay, coat still streaming, eyes closed. He wondered if she could hear them.

With grunts of effort, Newt wiggled her lame forepaw deep into the crack.

"She's close," said Fessran, peering down from the top. "Just a little bit more, Thistle."

Thakur saw Newt's lips draw back from her clamped teeth as she forced more of her leg in.

"You're touching now," came Fessran's voice from the top. "Spread your pad. Get your claws out."

Newt snarled and strained. She shot an agonized glance at Thakur. "Not strong enough. Claws won't go far enough."

Thakur swallowed, not knowing what to say. It wasn't her fault if her leg had not completely come back to normal. If it hadn't, she would never have been able to get in this far. But will could overcome weakness, if she wanted to free Ratha badly enough.

I can't condemn her if she fails, he thought. *But I won't be able to keep away the doubt.*

Newt gave a grunt, then a startled gasp.

"She's got a clawhold," Fessran said from the top. "Come up here and look."

Thakur bounded up beside the unconscious Ratha and peered down at Newt's rust-colored forepaw, lit by a stray beam of sunlight. She had one claw hooked into the side of Ratha's leathery pad. Thakur saw the tendons in Newt's foot stand out as she strained to spread her forepaw and extend the claws. She got another claw into Ratha's pad and then another.

"Pull slowly," Thakur called down to her. "Don't jerk, or you'll lose your hold." He heard her panting shallowly and knew her leg was cramping. Then he saw her foot starting to inch back, Ratha's paw moving with it. He suppressed his impulse to yowl at the sky. Instead he joined Fessran in trying to lick the salt water from Ratha's coat and lie across her to provide what warmth they could.

From his position atop the rock, he peeked down in the crack. Ratha's foot had stuck at a cluster of mussel shells in the crevice. Newt wriggled and panted but couldn't get past the obstacle. Slowly she unhooked her claws from Ratha's foot and began to scrape and pry at the shellfish, breaking away one fragment at a time. It was an agonizing effort for the weakened forepaw, but Newt kept doggedly at her task. Thakur started to call down instructions then stopped. No. He trusted Newt to do everything that was needed. He and Fessran should concentrate on reviving Ratha, getting her ready to move should Newt's efforts be effective.

They lay one on each side of her, warming her, trying to wring the water from her fur. Fessran scanned the sea anxiously for any sign that another wave was about to break over them.

Then Newt gave a yowl that was both triumph and pain as she snagged Ratha's foot again and pulled it free. Carefully Thakur got his jaws around the bruised and cut limb, gently drawing it out of the crevice.

"Thakur, another wave's coming," Fessran warned.

He wormed himself under Ratha's belly, heaved her up on his nape and shoulders, and half dragged, half carried her while yowling at Fessran to get Mishanti. He felt his load lighten slightly as Newt came up beside him and grabbed Ratha with her jaws. She was limping again, her leg drawn up and folded over in a fierce cramp. She grimaced with pain but said nothing as she helped Thakur carry Ratha away from the surging water.

The two hauled her to the highest spot on the island and then, when the water receded, wrestled her across the wave-washed boulders connecting this outermost islet with the chain leading back to the jetty. Fessran helped them as much as she could while carrying the cub.

Ratha, after being warmed and shaken around by her

short journey on top of Thakur, began to show some signs of life. Thakur took her a short distance to a hollow that screened out the wind. He laid her down on a slab that slanted at an angle, allowing water to drain from her fur instead of puddling around her.

Thakur and Newt began to lick her again, helped in their task by weak sunlight that grew stronger as the clouds parted. Her eyes remained closed, but her whiskers twitched and she whispered, "Thakur, I'm so numb I can't feel anything in my legs. Is my forepaw . . ."

He answered her unspoken question by pushing her limp foreleg toward her nose. "You've still got all your paws, thanks to your daughter."

He saw her rib cage rise then fall in a huge sigh of relief.

"Where's Thistle-chaser?" she asked, her eyes still shut. Thakur's gaze went to Newt, and he watched her ears flick nervously.

"Here," she answered, her voice thin with exhaustion and uncertainty.

Ratha's teeth chattered but she managed to say, "Lie down with me. I need you."

With another uncertain glance at Thakur, Newt arranged herself with her belly against Ratha's back. Thakur saw her grimace as her lame foreleg cramped. "Here," he said, taking her paw in his mouth and pulling it to ease the tight, knotted muscles. He massaged it gently with his tongue.

"Well this is certainly a cozy group," said Fessran as soon as she had dried Mishanti as well as she could. "I'm starting to feel left out."

"Well, join us," said Thakur. "Ratha needs all the warmth she can get."

"After what I did, I'm not sure . . ."

"She doesn't need apologies or arguments," Thakur replied. "Just a warm pelt against her."

"Mine's pretty damp, but I'll do what I can." Fessran shook herself off and fluffed her fur.

Together they rubbed against Ratha and wrung as much water out of her fur as they could by pressing against her. The sunlight brightened, helping to dry her pelt, while the sheltering rocks kept the wind from blowing away the heat.

Yet as Thakur worked alongside the others, he felt that there were many things yet to be resolved. As Ratha started to recover, Newt began inching away from her, as if she could only dare to touch Ratha when she was too sick or weak to really notice.

And as Ratha became more like her old self in the warmth and dryness of the sun and those around her, she seemed ill at ease with Newt. She let her daughter gradually retreat without calling her back. Perhaps, Thakur thought, everything that had happened on the island was just a feverish dream to her, unsure, unreal. And perhaps to Newt the intimacy that crisis allowed was gone.

He looked at Ratha and then at her daughter and felt angry. Both were strong, stubborn, and adamant about denying the tie that bound them together, yet both were clearly driven by it.

He shook himself, bristled his whiskers, and said, "Ratha, Thistle-chaser, there is someone I would like you to meet."

222

Both stared at him as if he had gone mad.

"What, by the Red Tongue's ashes, are you talking about?" asked Fessran. "There's no one else on this wave-washed rock but us."

He ignored the Firekeeper. Instead he went to Thistle-chaser, nudged her back toward Ratha. "This is your mother," he said, looking into the sea-green eyes. "She birthed you, fed you, and desperately wanted to love you."

He turned next to Ratha, still lying on her side, looking up at him. "And this is your daughter. She came from your belly, suckled at your teats, and never had the chance to be what you wanted her to be."

Pausing, he surveyed both of them. "That is the simple truth between you. You may deny it at the top of your voices, but everything you have done shows that it is still at work."

There was a very long silence.

Ratha lowered her muzzle, looking at the ground, then gave a sideways glance at Newt. "Thakur has the most sense of any of us, doesn't he? Do you think he's right?"

"He is right," said Newt softly, choosing her words carefully and slowly. "But want to know. Why you bite me bad when I was small?"

Ratha closed her eyes, and for an instant Thakur thought she couldn't answer the question.

"I think the best answer to that," Ratha said, "is to have Fessran bring Mishanti over here."

When the Firekeeper had placed the cub between Ratha and Thistle-chaser, Ratha said, "Look at him. If there is light in his eyes, it is hard to see, isn't it?" As the Firekeeper started to bristle, she added, "No,

Fessran. I'm not making a judgment of him now. For one thing, I'm hardly in a condition to do that. I just want to show Thistle-chaser something she needs to know." Ratha nudged Mishanti so that he faced Thistle-chaser.

"That is what you looked like to me," Ratha said. "I looked in your eyes and could not see what I wanted the most; the promise that you would grow up as one of the Named, be able to speak, think, and know what names mean." She looked up at her daughter, half-angry, half-pleading. "Can you understand? I had seen the empty faces of the Un-Named and to think that you would be like them . . . I couldn't bear it. I clawed Bonechewer. I bit you. I didn't realize it would wound you so badly. I didn't know."

Thistle-chaser bent her head and thoughtfully licked the collar of rough fur that hid her scar. Then she gave Ratha a searching look. "Am I what you . . . are afraid of?" she asked.

"I'm not sure," Ratha admitted.

"Am I what you wanted?"

"I'm not sure about that either," Ratha confessed. She looked away. "You lived so long without me, do you really care what I think?"

Newt looked as if she were struggling to put the right words together. At last she said, "I did not live without you. We both made Dreambiter."

Ratha's jaw trembled. "There is no way I can take back what I did. And I know you can't pretend it didn't happen. That trail is not an easy one."

"You do one thing for me," Newt said. "Help me let Dreambiter go."

"How?" Ratha's gaze went to Thakur. He could see the lostness in her eyes.

He answered, "The Dreambiter is everything in you that she dreads and fears."

"But I am not just that," Ratha said, pleading. "Thakur, tell her. I'm not."

"You will have to show her yourself. By not judging, not pushing, and learning patience."

Ratha looked away from him toward Newt. Nervously licking the tip of her nose, she gave a soft come-here purr. Newt crouched then crept to her, putting her head beneath Ratha's chin. Slowly, tentatively, Thakur saw Ratha lick the top of Newt's head. She gave a startled grimace. Obviously the sea had not rinsed away all of the sea-beast tang from Newt's fur. But she did not let the rhythm of her licking falter. She sent a defiant glance toward Thakur.

Then Newt withdrew her head and settled nearby, laying her head on her forepaws.

"I think this gives us a lesson about judging cubs," Thakur observed. "If we could be so wrong about Thistle-chaser, what about others? The thing we call the light in our eyes is more than just that. I think it shows itself in many ways and we must learn to see it in whatever form it takes."

He saw Newt twitch her tail impatiently. "What about him?" she said, pointing her nose at Mishanti.

"Well, I guess we should let him grow a little more; give him the chance that we didn't give you," Ratha answered.

"No," Newt said abruptly, startling everyone. She

rushed on, her anger making her strangely eloquent. "It won't work. He is like I was. Different. None of you will have the patience to teach him. You will always be thinking that he should be this or should be that. Even if you try not to, you will. And someone will get impatient and bite him."

Fessran narrowed her eyes at Newt. "Then what do you suggest?"

"Let me take Mishanti, teach him what I know."

The Firekeeper grumbled to herself, but Thakur heard Ratha say, "She's right. We would get impatient with him. Even you, Fessran."

"I'm not sure that she's the best . . ." Fessran started.

"Well, she may not be, but we certainly didn't do any better," Ratha argued. Then she turned to Newt. "I'd like you to come into the clan and help Fessran with Mishanti."

Thakur saw Fessran sit up, startled. "You mean you're not going to throw me out? Even after what I did?"

"No, singe-whiskers." Ratha grinned at her. "Who else can I depend on to tell me when I'm running the wrong trail? Thakur often knows, but his voice is sometimes too soft. Fessran's yowl I can't help but hear. Even if I do disagree."

"You may not have been entirely wrong," Fessran said softly, looking at Mishanti, who was frisking about with his tail. "He hasn't shown any ability to speak."

"Perhaps he doesn't need to." The interruption was Newt's. "I didn't. Not for long time. Perhaps he the same way."

"But words are important to us in the clan," Ratha

said. "And they are important to you now. I thought you wanted to come into the clan. There is no reason why we can't accept you."

Newt gathered herself together. "I don't want your clan. My seamares give me what I need. I want to be with you," she said, turning to her mother, "but as . . . friend, not leader."

Ratha's whiskers sagged a little. Thakur imagined that she thought Newt would be eager to end her long isolation and be welcomed back among the Named. But Newt's adversity had fostered a sense of independence that could not be given up easily.

"Let me take Mishanti," she said, looking at Ratha and Fessran. "Let me teach him to live with seamares. Let me keep my own ground and my own way and make my own choice to be with the Named or not. That is what I ask."

Thakur turned to the two, who were staring at each other with disgruntled looks.

"I hate to mention this," said Fessran, pointing toward the cub with her nose. The wound over his ribs had stopped bleeding and was crusted with dried blood. "You were the one who ripped up his side. Can I trust you?"

Newt looked down at her paws. "He is hurt. I was hurt. We both share that."

"I know, but is it . . ." Fessran began.

"This is part of letting the Dreambiter go," Newt answered.

"I think I understand what she means," Ratha said softly to Fessran. "I think she's right. It is the best way, though not the easiest." She addressed Newt again. "Since we have enough grazing and water for the herdbeasts to breed well, we can concentrate on the three-horns and dapplebacks, while you and Mishanti herd the seamares. Is that what you want?"

"Knock down the pen and let your seamares out," Newt said. "They can't live behind thorns and sticks. They need the beaches."

"She's right, Ratha," Thakur added. "The beasts aren't eating, and they'll soon get sick."

He could see that she disliked the idea of abandoning the pen after all the effort that had gone into making it. "Perhaps the seamares aren't the best animals for our purposes, and trying to pen them was a mistake," Ratha admitted. "We have what we need to survive. Yes, I will let them go, and you can live among them with Mishanti. I haven't been able to give you much, but at least I can give you that. Is it enough?"

"Yes." Newt bent down and touched noses with Ratha. "I am glad that my Dreambiter has become my mother," Thakur heard her hiss softly. She turned to Thakur. "Will you help me give the gift of words to Mishanti when the time comes?"

He felt himself grinning. "If you'll teach me to swim."

"Thistle, what about me?" Fessran asked, sounding forlorn. "I'd like to see him sometimes."

"You love Mishanti," Thistle-chaser said, facing the Firekeeper. "I turn to you if I feeling mad with him. Is enough?"

"I'll hold you to it," Fessran promised.

"Well, now that we've got all this sorted out," Thakur put in, "perhaps we should think about finding our way back before the tide comes in again. Ratha, can you walk?"

He watched her get shakily to her feet. She took a few steps, winced, and drew up her battered forepaw. "I'll limp, but I'll get there."

Newt came alongside her. "Use your hind legs more and bring them under you. Then you can take bigger steps."

Thakur saw Ratha give Newt an exasperated look, but she took the offered advice.

"Well, you can't deny she knows what she's talking about," he observed.

"Now you've got two of us," Ratha retorted, hobbling beside her daughter.

"Not for long. You've just got a sprain, and Newt's leg needs only a rest and a little more strengthening." He led the way, looking back as Ratha and Newt followed.

"If I see that wretched fish, I'll bite his tail off," Fessran growled through her mouthful of Mishanti's scruff fur. Then she padded after, starting the long up and down scramble and swim that would bring them back to the jetty.

The four made their way across the islands and at last regained the jetty by the time twilight was starting to fall. Above, clouds were gathering, and startled seamares honked at the bedraggled party, as Thakur, Ratha, Newt, and Fessran climbed along the spine of rock that led back to the beach. Ratha found herself lagging behind the others, even though they tried to slow down to her tired pace.

Newt did not want to return with them to the forested area where the Named had settled. Instead, she asked

Fessran for Mishanti, and when the Firekeeper reluctantly let him down, she picked him up by the scruff and padded away with him.

"That poor cub is going to be so confused by all of this," Fessran said.

"Stop worrying. She said you can visit him," Thakur answered.

The sky had been clouding over again. Ratha looked up as a heavy raindrop splashed down on her nose. Billowing gray clouds stretched across the sea and were rolling inland. Another raindrop struck her back. Soon the rain pattered down all around Ratha and her two companions as they crossed the beach, climbed the bluff, and made their way back to the forested pool beneath the cliff.

While Ratha soothed her bruised and aching foreleg in the pool, Thakur went off to collect Aree and Ratharee from the trees where they had been placed for safekeeping. Fessran yawned then climbed up to a slate-colored ledge, where she curled up out of the rain and fell asleep.

Ratha let her leg dangle in the pool, overhanging ferns and branches sheltering her. She smelled the storm, the cool, wet air, and the rain. This looked like a big storm: one that might move far enough inland to break the drought.

Before long Thakur arrived, bringing both treelings. Ratharee chirred with delight and took up her customary place on Ratha's shoulder.

"Listen," Ratha said, pricking her ears to the soft hiss of rain falling through the trees.

Thakur sat in the open, letting the downpour rinse sea salt from his coat. At last he shook himself off and lay down near Ratha. "If that keeps up, the streams will soon be running again on our old home ground," he said. "Are you thinking we might be able to return?"

"Not for a while. And I don't want to leave Thistle-chaser all alone again." Ratha laid her nose on one paw, extending the other to Thakur to have it skillfully licked and massaged.

"You were disappointed when she said she didn't want to join the clan."

Ratha grunted. "I was surprised. I thought she'd jump at the chance. Instead she turned her tail on it."

"She's impetuous, stubborn, and wants to do things her way. I'd be surprised if she wasn't. After all, she is your daughter." Thakur nibbled a toe-claw.

She is your daughter. The phrase whispered gently in her mind, blending with the sigh of the falling rain. *My daughter. One who is stubborn, willful, strong, self-reliant, and resourceful—and one to take pride in.*

It occurred to her that Thistle-chaser had changed something else as well. Bonechewer, her Un-Named father, had been Thakur's brother. If, as Thakur said, cubs from such matings had the same potential as those whose parents both came from the clan, even if their development was not as rapid, then perhaps such pairings might not be as risky as Ratha had once thought. She had already learned that there were individuals with worthy qualities among the Un-Named.

She closed her eyes, feeling Thakur's tongue soothe the ache from her leg. "Herding teacher, perhaps you won't need to go away when the next mating season comes."

He lay down next to her. "Would you be willing to accept another cub like Thistle-chaser?"

"What she might have been like if I hadn't turned on Bonechewer and bitten her . . ." Ratha sighed.

"She still has that chance," Thakur answered. "You know, Ratha, I sensed something about her that I don't understand. To us she seems slow, but I think she understands certain things in a way we don't. It's not just cleverness; it's something else. You know that our cubs take longer to grow up than the young of those creatures who don't think or speak. If Thistle-chaser and cubs like her grow even more slowly, perhaps it is not because they are less than we, but more."

Ratha rolled on her back, letting Ratharee scramble onto her chest. "That is an uncomfortable thought, Thakur."

"That seems to be the way of the Named, to think uncomfortable thoughts, to do uncomfortable things," said Thakur slowly. "But our feet are set on this path, and we can't turn aside. Nor would I want to." He stretched himself, groomed his back.

Ratha lay with her treeling on her chest between her raised forepaws. There had been two other cubs in the same litter that produced Thistle-chaser. Could either one of the siblings have survived? If so, what would they be like? Perhaps one day she would search for them and find out. It would be, as Thakur said, a difficult thing to do. But such an effort could bring its own reward, such as the quiet joy she felt now.

At last the old memories and pains could gradually be put to rest. The Dreambiter would fade away, for both Thistle-chaser and herself. A part of her life was passing behind now. She felt as though she had finished shedding an old coat and now wore clean, new fur. The weight of guilt from her past had slipped from her, making her feel airy and light.

The Named now had two homes: their old territory and this new place by the sea. And though their efforts to keep and tend the seamares had not turned out as well as they'd hoped, still the experience had enlarged their skills, allowing more choices. When the drought broke, some of the Named might return to clan ground, others might stay.

She thought about the future, what might happen with Thistle-chaser and Mishanti. Would the cub grow up as Fessran's vision had foreseen, to carry a torch burning brightly in his jaws and be a leader of the Named? Or would it be Thistle-chaser, scarred, but strangely gifted, who took over leadership when Ratha grew too feeble to guide the clan's way?

All this didn't matter now. What mattered was that she had found both a daughter and a wiser, better part of herself. The times to come might not be certain, but neither would they be shadowed with pain and guilt. She lay on her side, listening to the promise in the pattering rain. It was enough.